Airawnk:

Layers of Simulation

Science fiction

Fernando Fernandez

This book is especially dedicated to my mother, my family, and all my loyal readers for their unwavering support.

Table of Contents

I. Glitches

Why do people go on with their lives like nothing happened? They seem to be numb. Haven't they realized? Of what, Stephen? The world is changed! It's ruled by a system, and we are all programmed to go about our business in a certain way. Oh, come on! You are not a program in your head. Stop stressing about it. Have some fun! Yeah, right. You don't seem to understand what's going on, either! Megan, didn't you notice it? What now? A time jump! An earthquake? No, not that. It is a dimensional leap! Are you delusional? Of course not. I am the only one aware of these subtle changes.

A quantum leap is perhaps the best term to describe this growth that is disproportionate to what we have done so far. Post-war society has made extraordinary technological leaps. After the reverse engineering work, the whole world suddenly changed, and there was no clear explanation of where this unexpected knowledge came from. It has become an existence in society. It is not so easy to believe. Even our most brilliant scientists admit to getting their ideas from lucid dreams, from fantastic astral journeys into the light, from conversations in caves and mountains with angels and extraterrestrial beings... We are constantly growing and striving to get closer to success. To do this, we must keep in mind that the hardest thing we have to go through is to overcome our own programming and that of the system.

Stephen grabs Megan's arm and says, "I don't know what you are looking at. Everything is right in front of you." I can't see anything. The same goes for the simulations. He pushes her against the wall. I may be a little crazy again. However, it's the algorithms that make you repeat the same actions and routines. Let it go. Just let me go! You're hurting me. I'm sorry. I didn't realize the pressure I was putting on you. You're crazy.

What happens when we accept that change is real? In fact, what has happened in the decades of our civilization has advanced little in the millennia of human existence. Something will happen soon if you make any comparisons. Okay then. I expect quantum fusion any day now. What are you talking about? If you were the original Megan, would you understand me? I'm just saying you've changed. The random, non-deterministic evolution that a quantum system undergoes when measurements are made sporadically must be the result of an intervention. What kind of intervention? We should find out about it. However, the question should be, how does this collapse occur and how to measure it?

A "quantum leap?" Yes, it alludes to the realization that nature seems to violate informally formulated "principles." What is it? Nature does not create cracks or discontinuities. Who is responsible for the expected changes? Someone up there must be pulling the strings. It may be the most plausible explanation. For what? This nonsensical feeling, which is part of a different reality, perhaps another dimension. It is like a shifting vibration or an upgrade in our DNA. No, I haven't perceived it. Of course, she hasn't noticed anything at all. She's part of this masquerade. That's why she's quite different in this dimension. She used to be so shy, with a charming personality and so affectionate. Now, she's extrovert, disruptive, and absolutely careless!

Please knock it off, Stephen! You're such a worrisome fella! You need to learn to relax. I do so whenever I can. In fact, I exercise and meditate every day. Really? Yes, Megan! She laughs aloud. She seems to not know what I like or what I do. This is odd. Megan replied, "So do I. I do yoga. If you want, you can join me, Stephen." Thanks, that's really kind of you. Although I do not like bending over like a contortionist. You should remember that. Don't be silly, Steph! How did you call me? I called you Steph! Nobody does that, except for my mom. I am surely not your mom. Very funny! Her sense of humor is killing me. I hate it when she tries to crack a joke out of everything. I don't like to be around clowns, especially when they laugh at nothing really funny. What did you say? Nothing, darling. She smiled back at me. At least I made her happy. I loved her in the previous universe. However, here it's quite the opposite. My feelings are not so clear. Sometimes, I even think that I don't like her at all. This must have been done on purpose to drive me crazy. However, those memories come crashing through, like a whirlwind that takes me up and down.

And how do you know you exist, Megan? How do I know I exist? Why would you ask me to do something so obvious? If it is so obvious, surely you can answer it. I know I exist because I'm seeing you, I'm breathing. In short, I have a thousand sensations as a consequence of being here now. It sounds like a good argument. However, in a dream, you can also breathe and see around you. Thus, you have all the same sensations that awaken. Even though none of them is real. Therefore, you cannot trust your senses since they could be deceiving you, as in a dream, you can not support your existence in the sensations that you perceive with your body. Imagine Steph that you fall into the water off a boat and you don't know how to swim. You dive once, twice, and always kick and come up and look for oxygen. On the surface, you are by instinct looking for a breath of air. You don't see it. However, it's there and it is what we breathe. Don't tell me it doesn't exist. If the sun does not exist, go out to the desert, or go to the arctic; your senses will not deceive you. We know what threatens our existence and we instinctively react to it. Programming or not, the risk is there.

What if you can't make an empirically based argument, does it have to be a rational argument? Yes, indeed. However, let's make it more interesting. Now, Megan, imagine that there is an evil genius, a divinity, a super-advanced alien, or a being from another dimension. Whatever you prefer, this being is making us believe that every rational argument is true, even though it is not. For example, convincing us that simple math operations are incorrect when they are not. In other words, I cannot make an empirical argument because my senses will deceive me, but neither can I make a rational argument because the genie will deceive me too. Why do you assume that someone is going to go to the trouble of monitoring over seven billion extremely complicated human beings? It is really absurd and counterproductive. A being with such mental development and technology would design a program, an algorithm with artificial intelligence or something more advanced for such purposes and just watch as we destroy ourselves or build something better as a civilization.

With my hands tied, how do you think I am going to solve the question of whether I exist? What are you looking for, Steph? I'm looking for an unshakable first principle for my philosophy, and I think I've got it. Now I will continue with my argumentation; as you rightly say, I cannot make an empirical argument, since I would doubt whether my senses are deceiving me, nor can I make a rational argument, since I would doubt whether an evil genius or some divinity is deceiving me. It would seem that I could not be sure of anything with those restrictions. Nevertheless, if there is one thing I cannot doubt, it is that I am doubting. Therefore, if I am doubting, I am thinking, and if I am thinking, therefore I exist.

Such reasoning can be used in reverse too. You do not exist, Steph! Prove it to me! You see that all your arguments are futile and you only want to corner me with syllogisms and phrases as stale as official science, so stop the philosophical peroration so old, with logic somewhat surpassed by science. The limitations of our senses have been compensated for by our technology. Are we any closer to proving whether or not there is simulation? It is possible, more than ever before in human history. You have already proved me right. I dare you to punch that wall. If this is a simulation and you don't exist, it won't hurt! However, Megan, that's irrational. Sure, just like all your arguments, and if it will hurt, it will be just a perception of your touch and your nervous system. Pain exists. However, suffering does not. How so? Suffering is a creation of our minds.

Simulation can exist in concrete environments as real as the wall, Steph. For instance, the sun, the moon, and others. It does not imply the elimination of concrete structures. We print in 3-D with concrete materials to turn something abstract from our screen, a concept or idea into an alternate, different reality. We have even printed functional organs and parts for our body. All that is necessary is the genetic material for such purposes. They go from illusion or mind to creation. The same goes for the manufacture of cyborgs, robots, androids, robotic pets, and artificial intelligence. There is a fine line between simulation and reality, video games and virtual environments; the abstract and the concrete are beyond human perception.

Sometimes you just have to make others believe you go on with your programming and that monotony and boredom do not alter you; on the contrary, they are your usual partners that do not distract you from work and family affairs. These stories of common people can still make them think you are a law-abiding citizen and part of the regular population. That entertains them while you are achieving your real goals, unmasking the system of this fake world. When we are not sleeping, we live in stress or survival mode. It accounts for approximately two thirds of our lives. When we are asleep, which is one third of our lives, we are calm and in a very different vibration. We can reprogram ourselves minutes before falling asleep at night and early in the morning, a few minutes after we wake up. Our subconscious can help us to reprogram ourselves in a better way.

Have you ever heard of the "Mandela Effect?" No, I haven't. Why? Some believe that this effect is evidence of the existence of multiple dimensions in the universe. How has everything changed? The situation today is very different. For a long time, more and more people have lived similar experiences on several continents. What's more, many strange things are happening, especially around the world. Our personal situation is fake! This is infallible! This "evidence" is immersed in another dimension. There are multiple cases to validate my premises. We have to communicate with "Dimension Jumpers" via video calls. Our first case is ready. Here's Alex. Hello, how are you? Well, thanks for letting me share my experience. I'll say no more. What happened? I was in a supermarket when a man who wanted to sell lottery tickets came up to me and said, "I got your license plate number 8! However, my license plate number is 20. I've been using it for a long time on that number. Is this your vehicle? Yes, just in front of you. It is a metallic blue SUV. How could I forget it? It felt weird to go over there and make sure the guy was right. This is outrageous! Calm down! He said, "Will you buy me a ticket?" I didn't answer him and walked away stunned. It was as if somebody had touched my most precious treasure, something very private that I didn't remember now. I looked at the registration document and it was indeed a new number. How did it change? It was like being in an unknown dimension. The second case is a weirder one. Hello, welcome Adria! Hello, thank you for your consideration of my case. What happened to you? After lunch, I took a nap. It was a busy weekend, and I was a little tired from work. What do you do for a living? I'm a model and an actress. How nice! What happened next puzzled me. I woke up a little late and looked at the clock and saw that it was 30 minutes prior to falling asleep. I checked the time on other clocks, and even on the Internet. And I didn't understand how that was possible. How do you know the time when you have fallen asleep? Thus, I went to rest at the end of a call, and the time is recorded on my phone. You can see it here. I can't change that. Of course not. Everyone in the house was as scared as I was.

A few years ago, a giant particle accelerator opened a black hole, activated a corresponding wormhole, and entire planets were sucked into another dimension, causing time to pass faster and the days to get shorter every year. All this is the focus of all sorts of unimaginable speculation.

A particle physics experiment that seemed to go smoothly in 2012 coincides with the end of the Mayan calendar, when the apocalyptic cataclysm becomes a simple transition to another dimension, a quantum leap without earthquakes or rudeness. changed. I thought these were pure conspiracy theories and had no scientific value. The nuances of both worlds are developing and increasing day by day. In fact, they caused significant changes in our universe, tilting the planetary axis and accelerating global heat sensation more than predicted, "he said. You won't notice it. However, your work depends on it. It is based on the study of quantum and subatomic matter; consequently, it focuses on observing how astronomers see stars. The existence of atomic subparticles facilitates the exploration of the multiverse, black holes, dark matter, dark energy, alternate dimensions, spiritual realms, or unknown worlds. They are free to fantasize as far as our imagination can take us. This desire to reach other realities does not necessarily have to be associated with the spiritual, as it is intertwined with matter. A leap in science beyond the simple recognition of altered or distorted physical reality. Accessing and experiencing the real physical world directly through a physical body is just one example of how immersive simulation interfaces can be. If so, what's the difference between believing in something and living it? What's stopping you from changing your current situation? Welcome to a quantum leap, Megan.

Perhaps the most disturbing thing about this quantum scientific revolution is not its chaotic and almost unpredictable behavior. However, its desire to break with simulation by doing something as simple as the Mandela effect: it is a feeling. Change it! It is the separation of ourselves personally and emotionally from what surrounds us. Because what you perceive as "reality" is just a mental structure. That leap to another level is for those who want to get to a smarter, freer, and more complete world, to be able to talk to animals, improve their physique, improve their health, and more.

Megan asks, "What do you know about the mirror technique?" This consists of looking at yourself on a reflective surface until you cross the barrier and start to find yourself on the other side. Is that possible? I don't know. I've never tried it. Don't assume that what random people are posting on social media is true. You're right! Although it may be achievable. There is also a way to transfer liquids between two containers. You go from science to magic. Yes. I think so. Have your subjective views changed? You are not changing your physical body for another. However, the dimensional shift has altered your genes and modified some of your physical and cognitive traits. It is as if many humans are empty replicas of those who existed in previous dimensions.

The third dimension jumper is already with us. How are you, Tony? Thank you very much. I am a person aware of the transition to another dimension. What happened? I couldn't find the medicine I needed. My wife told me to call the drugstore. However, they had run out of them. Later, I went to the airport. I got on a plane to go to a business meeting abroad. I felt like I was struck by lightning when I was on the plane. The stewardess tells me, "Don't worry, everything will be fine." I woke up early at home. Then I opened the medicine drawer in my room and took out the medicine. I have no wife in this dimension. Look for her everywhere. No one knew her. It's as if she never existed. Since then, there has always been evidence of the Mandela effect: false memories of family events or movie quotes. Are the movies different here too? Yes, even the music. Another change I have experienced is that the next day in this dimension, I no longer needed these pills.

A fourth jumper is happy to share the details of her case. Keep it up, Vanna! I was on the verge of an accident when a car coming towards me at high speed and without brakes threatened to run me over. I closed my eyes and nothing happened to me. It was just a close call. The other vehicle had gone off the road over a hill. Everyone said it was great. One woman said to me, "It wasn't your turn to die today." I thought I wouldn't be able to have children. However, the day after the accident, I went for a routine checkup and they recommended a pregnancy test. I told my doctor I was single. He said, "It doesn't matter." After that, the results showed I was pregnant. I had no boyfriend, and in the previous universe I was not fertile. How was that possible? No one believed me. Now, on this other level, my child is at your disposal. It's a dimension where you can jump on the day of the accident.

The fifth volunteer is ready to share her experience. Thanks, Abby, for being with us. Thank you for including me in your research. What was that you called "an eye-opener?" It was just like a flashback. I was at the mall. I saw a woman with a long white dress knocking at the glass door. What was odd about it? I knew exactly what she was going to do or say. I've seen or lived that before. How did you feel? I got goosebumps!

Some scientists believe they have discovered a quantum leap to another dimension and are being shown the truth of life. They believe that, at least on a spiritual level, jumpers have reached a level of consciousness that places them in a privileged, almost sacred place. The more aware I am of this process, the greater the connection with cosmic consciousness. I now have friends and family I know who remember certain events we lived through together. I have also noticed a change in their appearance; it is very strange that their faces look like clones instead of my people. I have been working to continue to grow towards enlightenment by disconnecting emotionally from everything, people, and work at all levels.

I must find out what the matter is. This uncertainty is driving me crazy. A "simulated reality" is the claim that computers can simulate reality to the extent that it is indistinguishable from "true" reality. It would involve conscious minds that may or may not know how to live in a simulation. You need to disentangle your mind to open up a whole new world of possibilities.

Errors in the simulation are spontaneously detected and come in many forms, such as white noise, freezing of images, and free space in areas where no error should occur, such as the sky or air. There is also a boring world that offers no variants or identical unrelated people in the same routine. How is it that reality is not so real and can always be something else? Scientists believe that the universe around us may not be real.

Matrices, grids, orders, or imperfections of systems have become common references. We are dealing with parallel worlds and alternative timelines in a universe in which we are actors in a play whose scripts were written and decorated by someone else. However, it is often not enough; again, we only access parts of reality through our limited senses, while the truth remains hidden using special devices developed in recent years, such as microscopes, telescopes, infrared and ultraviolet vision.

In addition, little has been done to increase the knowledge of the truth about other devices! Only after infinite repetitions of the same action, thanks to a "mistake" indicating that something is wrong with the structure of reality. Either it is not as solid as it seems, or it shows that you are in a completely different reality. We live in a computer simulation. Or it could be in the head of a gigantic being. The idea of computer simulation appeals to the language we can speak today, using the metaphors that technological reality offers us. In other words, it is a metaphor that opens the door to an idea rather than something that can be physically described by building blocks such as computers, connections, binary languages, networks, and nodes. As a result, our reality is a simulation created by someone else, and the projection belongs to them. And it is also a logical consequence of other basic metaphors we humans rely on: life is like a journey. It's like waking up in a dream; we leave one dimension and travel to another; from one world to the other. So, the idea of a simulation is, above all, a way of expressing the basic feeling that the world is not exactly what it seems. There is more to it than meets the eye.

The social implications of this theory are vast. What about living in a world where virtual reality is at some point indistinguishable from "real" reality per se? The perceptual dimension provides more impressive information. The feeling of living in a simulated reality is accessible through the experience of the body and its seemingly fixed boundaries dissolving, changing, or simply being unexplainable.

What are the faults in reality or in the simulation that may mean that we live in a simulation? Glitches in Reality? What do you mean? A completely simulated universe? Simulation? Yes, you seem to be more programmed and asleep than most. You are opening my eyes to a dimension completely unknown to me. That is exactly what this is about; making others aware of what we do and how we can progress as a human collective. Our life is not a perfect system. Should it be? Of course it should! You haven't noticed that we are surrounded by perfection at the highest level? What exactly do you mean? Can you give me an example to understand your point of view? For instance, the sun is at a distance that does not burn or freeze us, or if you prefer, our planet is in the goldilocks zone. We have a satellite, the moon, just one, not dozens like other planets. Our moon is far enough away to have a tug of war that allows us to enjoy the tides and a perfect balance. Yes, and it also makes us lunatics. Stop joking. A perfect atmosphere, breathing air, magnetic shield, different barometric pressure on land and in the deep sea, ozone layer against ultraviolet rays, a moderate gravity that allows the human body to develop, enough drinking water to support life, plants, and animals for food, a regal Earth, day and night, seasons, northern lights, clouds, wind, rain, and so much diversity of life that it's frightening. None of this would exist if we varied our location a bit. Where are you going with all this? This is not random, not trial and error. Do you think there is a divine creator? I don't know if it's divinity or just a really advanced mind that has created everything you see below and above. Do you think it's a living thing? It may be possible. I think that perhaps we live inside it; or more likely, it's an artificial superintelligence that has been the only thing left of a mega-advanced "God" level civilization. How do we check it out? That's what I'm working on now. Count me in, Stephen. Thank you very much, Naim. I need all the scientific support I can get to solve this great mystery. No thanks at all, let's put our hearts into it and get to work. You've made me dizzy with so many hypotheses and speculations. You and your witticisms.

We live in a finite world of limited resources. We are beings of flesh and blood. We are the result of cosmic dust; particles vibrating at a certain frequency, which are held together by gravity with a quasi-celestial rhythm. Naim said, "There is no solid scientific evidence that we live in a nonsensical alternate reality that we have created. What I do believe is that people nowadays have a lot of imagination and free time."

A simulated reality is the proposition that suggests that reality could be a simulation, perhaps by a high-end quantum supercomputer belonging to a generation of artificial intelligence far off in the future, to a degree indistinguishable from "true" reality as it includes augmented reality, virtual reality, perceived concreteness, and pareidolia, among other variables. In addition, there are doubles for every person. There are up to seven similar people, almost the same, without any kinship. The universe tends to repeat itself to fill gaps and holes in the simulation, as well as the same patterns are followed.

An advanced simulation would contain conscious minds that may or may not know that they are living inside a simulation. Do we have free will in this simulation? I think we can fight for it. If this is your strongest version, what do you mean by that? Only the "simulation hypothesis" states that it is possible, and even very likely, that we are actually living in such a simulation. That is, a reality within the simulation. It has nothing to do with virtual reality, which is easily distinguishable from the experience of "true" reality; participants never doubt the nature of what they experience. Simulated reality, on the other hand, would be difficult or impossible to distinguish from "true" reality. And how did you figure it out then? Even perfection can have flaws and gaps that indicate it has reached its operating storage capacity; for example, upgrading a processor that can no longer handle all of the operations we now perform can be difficult due to the time required, and the software upgrade can be restricted to new users born after a certain date. Okay, sir. Well, what else could you tell us that it is a simulated reality or an imperfect simulation of what we believe is reality? When reality freezes in front of your eyes, when time seems to slow down, it is like the temporary memory of your computer is insufficient for the number of operations you are performing at the moment. You have loaded many heavy programs that require the use of a lot of memory. Neither the cloud nor the servers providing the simulated reality are sufficient for the level of civilization we have reached.

Maybe we were created to fail before this development. How so? What was implicit in our nature at the moment of creation, self-destruction? We are violent, aggressive, belligerent. We create wars, we destroy the planet. In short, we are not meant to go that far. There are loopholes in our program, though. Can we challenge our creator? Not with our current level of progress. However, if we become an intergalactic civilization or more than that, we may be able to create our own universe and see everything very differently.

The idea of a simulated reality encompasses several issues. Is there a difference between a simulated reality and a "real" reality? That is what we are trying to demonstrate, not just perception or intuition, basing ourselves on science to conclusively show everyone the programming of a certain algorithm in which we live, the very fiber where the zeros and ones are exposed in space-time. How should we behave if we knew we lived in a simulated reality? Act differently, be aware of the simulation, how to influence it and reject the destructive programming assigned to us. What you call fate, luck, or divine will is nothing more than the algorithm of the system. Yes, you are programmed to do or achieve certain things. It is your task to get out of it and become aware of it so you can challenge it and change it on your behalf.

Each view of the simulated reality can be considered as a potential scheme within each simulation at the same time. That is, they could all be possible, or they could be descriptions of the same thing that could support the existence of all of them. In a brain-computer interface simulation, each participant enters from the outside and connects his or her brain directly to the simulation computer. The computers send sensory data to him and interpret his desires and actions as responses. In this form of simulation, participants interact with and receive feedback from the simulated world. Competitors can even be recalibrated to temporarily forget that they are in the virtual world, i.e., "breaking the veil." Within the simulation, on the other hand, the participant's consciousness is represented by an avatar that may differ from the participant's actual appearance. To communicate effectively with the brain, we must create or discover codes or sequences to transmit information between the speaking and listening parts of the brain.

Some extreme advocates of simulation and at the same time insane "flat-earthers" say that the south of our planet does not exist and that actors are used to impersonate its inhabitants. When that fails, virtual people. In a virtual person simulation, each resident is native to the world being simulated. They have no "real" body in external reality, and their consciousness is limited to programming or assigned algorithms. Rather, each is a fully simulated entity with an appropriate level of consciousness implemented using the simulation's own logic, its own physics. In this way, they were downloaded from one simulation to another, or even archived in this pseudo-reality after death and revived at a later date. It is also possible for a simulated entity to be completely removed from the simulation by transferring its mind to a composite. Another way to draw a virtual reality inhabitant from a simulated world is to take a synthetic or virtual DNA sample, 'clone' the entity, and create a "real" world from that model. As a result, the "mind" of the being is not removed from the simulation. However, the body may have originated in the real world. A virtual being in a virtual world where the external reality is simulated separately from the artificial consciousness. A solipsistic simulation is one where consciousness is simulated, realizing that the "world" in which it participates exists only within one's own mind. Our reality is a simulation, and although there is more than a 50% chance of dying, our consciousness lives on in a simulated reality designed to test the simulator's strategies.

It is possible for advanced god-like civilizations to create computer simulations involving individuals with artificial intelligence. Such a civilization may run many, perhaps billions, of such simulations, just for fun, research, or some other reason. The individuals simulated within the simulation are not necessarily aware that they are within it. They live their daily lives in what is considered the "real world". In addition, it is possible that civilizations involve individuals with some form of artificial intelligence.

Part of the simulated nature of reality is also recognizable through video games, arguably one of the experimental and speculative sources that serve as the basis for simulation theory. As our games become more and more real, we can hypothesize and take for granted that the realities that create computerized versions of our game scenarios are themselves creations of others. These are more than just good guesses and explanations about virtual reality. We live in an artificially created digital reality. Investigating the impact of simulations on everyday life is devastating because it influences individual behavior and causes mass hysteria. One of them is that only they get it right, while everyone else is asleep or alienated from what is going on around them, and the purpose of the various conspiracy theories is to heighten the feeling of being awake in the reality that is presented. Reality is not measured by what we speculate. Although it is by what it means to others. Even if we agree to live in a simulation, the question remains the same: "How do I deal with this person I love?" How do you deal with this person who is my enemy? They are a consideration of the deep empathy needed in a world where attention is always being directed in a thousand different directions and in a world of solipsism that seems inevitable.

On the other hand, when reality itself collapses, simulation theory also acts as an escape route. Virtual reality has recurring fissures through which it returns to a fundamentally broken reality. The launch of simulation does not lead to a better world. The reality they access and "wake up to" is fundamentally

destroyed. "Real reality is very similar to a battlefield."
The most important thing for me is probably that we
have crossed the taboo, we have passed the point of no
return."
The feeling that our life is a confused life, even though
it may seem more or less in the near future. And what
we can learn, imagine, and create is the way we live in
these ruins, radically reinventing who we are.
Simulation theory is also a way of imagining this huge
movement around humanity, living in a reality full of
mistakes and failures. And failure is open both to the
discovery that reality is not "reality" and, if there is
the reality of "reality," it is not the promise of Eden
that has not changed. This is a recurring image in
popular culture. Some dimensions are an unstable
and unacceptable world, where mistakes accumulate
until the constructed and simulated characters and
associated human costs are revealed, and the people
who live there are deprived of their will. There is no
such thing as free will. When the world is annihilated,
the only place to return to is the same desolate world.
The only difference is the ability and willingness to
make choices.
If there is a way out of such a reality, simulation
theory can serve as an excuse, not through denial of
reality, even if the denial is to escape the feared
situation. Stephen tells Megan, "In part of my life, I
experienced the unreality that underlies simulation
theory." Those with brain problems? Not insanity,
honey, that's called schizophrenia. I got to the point
where I didn't want to get stuck with the idea that this
was all wrong, because there was an easier way to do
it. Is there such a thing as simulation or not? Of
course, not everything is simulated. There are things

that we feel are tangible and solid, and they are. Imagine a 3D printer with titanium elements as the base material for printing. Everything is simulated on your computer until the push button is pressed and the task of creating and sculpting the character on the screen begins. When it's done, it's solid and genuine. If you hit it, you will get hurt.

I think it's your most complete and specific statement about the world, reality, and the world superimposed on other worlds. Make it impossible to discriminate against even if there is one person who is the source of the others. Can you tell the difference between the design on your computer and the titanium model on your printer? Of course, that's clear. If you have the same opportunity to see both realities at the same time, you don't have to complain about sleeping or being programmed by a higher level of structure. It can be a complete simulation, or it can be understood as an invitation to unexpected discoveries to continue the wonderful journey of life itself. However, this requires a minimum of psychological integrity, self-awareness, and judgment.

Are you really me too? Some physicists, cosmologists, and other scientists today are reassured by the possibility that we all live in huge computer simulations. Of course, we instinctively object to this. It's so real that you can't think of it as a simulation. Furthermore, you should give some thought to the incredible advances that have been made in computing and information technology over the past decades and thousands of years. Computers have brought us incredibly realistic games and engaging virtual reality simulators. It is more than enough to be paranoid. How to distinguish between reality and simulation? And is it really important where we live? The universe is an experiment! Artificial intelligence and robotics experts suggest that our entire universe could be a high school student's science experiment in another universe. "When formed, a unique spacetime bubble is created. The resulting universe, although created by artificial processes, is completely real. Or at least, that is our perception. The idea that we are part of the simulation has prominent supporters, such as government officials and billionaire businessmen. The chances of us living in an objective reality are "one billionth." We are physical beings trapped in a false reality. Or there are at least two ways in which the universe around us cannot be real. In contrast, the second scenario held by many personalities is that humans are completely simulated beings. It suggests that it's just information manipulated by a large computer, like a video game character. There is no escape route in this universe. This is where we live and our only chance to live. Despite that, why do you believe in this tremendous potential? The answer is simple. We are already recreating the world through virtual reality. It not only simulates video games but also scientific research. You successfully created a virtual entity that shows signs of consciousness. Really? Of course, we developed our own consciousness, recreated the laws of physics, added variables we didn't know about, and created artificial intelligence, such as predicting the movement of objects with absolute precision. It is difficult to identify whether these entities are real or virtual. Soon, we plan to develop a lot of simulations that go beyond the "real" world.

So isn't it possible that intelligent beings in another corner of the universe have already reached that point? It seems quite plausible, given how far away other civilizations are. A virtual world where intelligent civilization never evolves to a sufficient level to generate these simulations, as it can self-destruct before reaching full evolution. The civilization used to be able to run these simulations, even though for some reason they chose to abandon them or leave them to fate. Abandoned due to a lack of interest in the person. How cruel!

An even more overwhelming possibility is that we live in a simulation. We are like the inhabitants of an ant farm. It is true that humanity has faced many problems due to the rapid development of industry and technology in recent years. For instance, climate change, nuclear weapons, and the possibility of mass extinction are all factors. However, no one needs to be definitive. Moreover, there is nothing to suggest that truly detailed simulations, in which agents experience themselves as real and free, are fundamentally impossible. Given that knowledge of the existence of other planets has come to mankind, it is hubris to believe that we are the smartest in the universe. One of the reasons for running simulations today is to better understand the real world in which we are supposed to live, to improve ourselves and to save lives. These are ethically indisputable reasons to continue recreating life. It does not exclude cloning, simulating the universe and continuing to explore the virtual world, which is often confused with reality itself.

Probably in simulation. How to prove it? One way to see if we are participating in a simulation is to look for errors in the program that generates the errors. For example, one might find contradictions in the laws of physics. Artificial intelligence experts suggest that you can also find errors by rounding computer numbers. Whenever an event has multiple possible outcomes, their probabilities must add up to one. If not, something must be wrong. For other scientists, the evidence that we are in a virtual reality is in the universe itself. Everything is perfectly aligned. Even small changes in the forces of nature can turn atoms into unstable particles or make life on Earth impossible. The macrocosm has a very similar shape to the microcosm, and it is the quantum universe that changes. It is only the laws of physics that govern this strange and stochastic universe. Quantum mechanics has come up with all sorts of weird things. For example, both matter and energy look granular. It looks like pixilation on the screen when viewed from a close distance. Another strong argument is that the universe seems to be acting mathematically like a computer program. Nevertheless, this argument seems to bite the tail. When superintelligence performs simulations in its own "real" world, it will probably follow the physical principles that govern the universe, just as we do now. In this case, our world is not mathematical because it is controlled by a computer, and so is the "real" world. In any case, finding solid evidence that we are in the simulation is very difficult, if not impossible. Our minds are not prepared to undertake the task or yet do it. We may never know because we do not have the technology to do so. Finally, in simulation, instead of overriding the rule, we design the agent to operate within the rule. Reality is quantum. At the end of this discussion, there is an idea that might alleviate the anxiety of determining whether it is just information being manipulated by a huge computer. For some physicists, this is the real world anyway. Quantum theory is increasingly couched in terms of information and computation. Other experts believe that the most basic level of nature may not be pure mathematics. However, pure information like zero or computer zero. Would you like to reduce it to simple binary code? Megan, are you offended? More like let me down.

Everything that happens upwards from particle interaction is calculated somehow. Examining the internal organs of the universe, the structure of matter on the smallest scale reveals that they are just a bit of local digital manipulation. This will take you to the heart of the problem. When reality is just information, we are like bits, quibits, tetrabits, neither more nor less "reality," whether in simulation or not. In any case, what we can do is provide information. Is every person you see a computer construct processing data encoded by your own consciousness? Partly, it is impossible to keep that image in mind for long. And that the only concept of reality worth having is what we experience and not the virtual world beyond. It's not as simple as taking an old philosophical critique and disguising it as technology. This doesn't hurt anyone; it just makes you question your own assumptions and prejudices. However, until it is shown that the difference between what we experience and "reality" leads to the difference between what we observe and act upon, our conception of reality doesn't change much. Do some ancient scientists claim that they already knew the universe was just an illusion? Yes, and those who try to challenge this idea object to me. There will always be energetic budding scientists who will refute this idea and scream that they will kick rocks and roll on the ground out of stubbornness and shortsightedness. How do we know that we are not living in a simulation? One of the oldest philosophical questions is whether the real world exists. We can only see things as perceived. Recognition of an object does not mean that the object is essentially real. Reality is a product of consciousness, and perception does not require belief in an object that exists independently of the perceiving subject. This does not make sense when we look at the workings of our minds. The brain creates conceptual ideas that reflect concrete objects, smells, tastes, images, etc., that we feel with our five senses. The veracity or accuracy with which this is done can be misleading, whether it matters or not, as we tend to automatically fill in the blanks with what we know or are familiar with.

This way of looking at the world is somewhat extreme and, in my opinion, can be disproved by what I call a "painful demonstration of the existence of objects." For instance, I walk down the street and see a cardboard box lying on the ground. I kick it with all my might; I break my foot because it turns out that there was an iron anvil inside the box. Evidently, if the universe were a mere creation of my mind, the stone would not have been there. That's a simplistic way of looking at things. However, let's not sing victory so soon. Just because you have the real world doesn't mean you know what it is. What we call the "real world" is actually in our heads and consists of a brain interpretation of data obtained through our senses, so the apple I see red is brown to the weak. Which is correct? Neither or both. What we call the real world is actually the world we perceive. The fact that many more people see the red apple than the brown apple does not imply that my perception is any more accurate than that of the colorblind. Let us not forget that the apple can have various shades of its skin and is not 100% red, and inside it is white. In summary, what we call the real world is a subjective experience of something that exists outside of us. However, we cannot experience directly, that is, without the intermediation of our senses and our brain processes, and if we could go beyond the little we reach of the light spectrum, colors that we do not even suspect that they exist, then our perception of the apple could change, as we do when we see a galaxy with a regular telescope, and then when we see it with an ultraviolet or infrared device, our perception changes because we have more information. Thus, what we need are sensors for more information. Improving our senses and bodies in general could bring us closer to a closer understanding of the universe and ourselves. More subtle are the theories that do not deny the reality of the external world. However, grant it a vicarious existence, as if pinned on pins. For them, our reality would be no more than a pale reflection of the world of ideas, which is the really existing one. They speak of conventional truth and absolute truth. In the everyday world, we act as if things exist intrinsically; it works in everyday life. Nevertheless, absolute truth tells us that things have no intrinsic existence; they are nothing but bundles of relations.

The poetic version of the unreality of the external world compares it to dreams, just as we live violently in dreams when we sleep and realize that there is no reality when we wake up. Life could have been similar. If the mind deceives us in the dream world, why shouldn't we deceive ourselves in the waking world? In the age of virtual reality, these philosophical books are adapted to postmodern times that has taken on a sympathetic tone. The reasoning is logical. However, it is still isolated. It would be interesting to know if there is any empirical evidence that we live in a simulation. Some arguments for living in a simulation are simply baffling. The universe appears to be based on mathematical principles. Physical phenomena such as black holes are discovered through equations long before they are physically discovered.

What's more, the principle of quantum uncertainty means that we can only calculate the probability that an electron is at a particular location. To know where it actually is, you have to observe it, and at that point, it will show you where that electron is in all possible space. This effect makes you think about what happens in video games and what is likely to happen in simulations. Like in actual video games, probably only what the protagonist needs in detail will be generated in the simulation to save resources. For example, in the flat earth theory, there is no Australia or Chile. Their inhabitants are actors. Knock it off!

In other words, what happens with quantum uncertainty is that computers don't increase the level of detail until we see electrons as we get closer to the location. Explain quantum uncertainty in a way that everyone can understand. Imagine a game where you walk into a room. The guys inside came up with something that I had to guess by asking questions that could only be answered with a yes or no answer. Now it turns out that the guys inside decided to play with me; they didn't think of that. The first question randomly answers my question, and the following questions do the same, with the only caveat that their answers cannot contradict the previous one. In other words, something does not exist. However, it is my research that shapes it.

Additionally, the idea of some physicists is that the ultimate building blocks of reality are fragments of information. Material things are nothing more than the result of information. What about units smaller than bits at the quantum level? Deciphering simulated reality. A gene can be seen as a physical substance that encodes information. Nevertheless, it is unimaginable for that information to create a gene.

Finally, Planck particles seem to define the lower limits of space. It could not be divided into smaller pieces. Does it make you think of anything? Indeed! into pixels!

Regardless, I think it's more plausible to live in the real world than in a simulation. What's your point, Megan? My claim is Occam's razor, that of the two hypotheses, the simpler one is always the true one. To accept that I am living in the real world, I must accept the Big Bang, and prior to that moment, another universe died and boom, ours start its birth. The formation of the solar system, the emergence of life, and the evolution of consciousness. Since I live in a simulation, in addition to all of the above, I have to assume the civilization that developed the computer that can create the simulation of the universe. I think it's easier to believe in the first option. You simplify everything and leave the discussion!

I have this feeling of an upshift. It all started...
Someone shouts, "Hurry, they are coming." I asked,
"Who's coming?" They are the ones. Who? The
shapeshifters!
Hey, Megan. Yes, what's all that hype, Steph?
Scientists next door detected a galaxy with 12 identical
copies. They call it the "sunburst" galaxy. A cosmic
clone that is self-copying. That's bizarre. It took place
really far away from our galaxy. Let's talk to them.
When they approached the group of geeks, they were
sharing notes. It took place really far from our cosmic
neighborhood. How did these twelve copies appear?
How many fake twin galaxies can we find out there?
There are still too many questions to be answered,
and we are just scratching the surface of this huge
cosmic iceberg. Steph interrupted them, "It's a
simulation!" They were all in awe. However, nobody
even attempted to dismiss his comments. They know
him very well and his reputation as a first-class
astrophysicist.
Nevertheless, the idea was caressed by Sydney, a
friend of his. The rest of the crew was not willing to
jump on the bandwagon. Megan wanted to ignite the
discussion. She said, "Doppelgangers, similar cities,
and repetitive patterns are not other things than
filling the voids, not errors in the system. Why are
there supposedly eight to nine people like you in this
world? Why is there a repetitive pattern, or is it our
brain that fills the blanks with familiar knowledge?
Why is this galaxy self-replicating? Is it a nursery
galaxy? They all looked at her, and even though they
ignored the previous questions, they went right on
asking her, "What did you mean by "nursery galaxy?"
A mother galaxy that creates its own clones to

populate this baby universe as it expands. Haven't you realized we are in an incipient soaring world? You ask questions and nobody has the answers. Not as of yet. Steph and Megan got back to their research. I won't talk about "déjà vu," the feeling of having experienced a present situation. It's odd, some kind of strange human phenomenon. Don't ignore birthmarks. Why? They may signal the cause of death in a previous life. Don't be silly! No, I am not superstitious at all. You've got to be kidding. It's odd. Have you ever dreamed of somebody you don't know, and then magically a few weeks later you run into that person? Gosh! I may have really crept out. Is there a Mandela effect hunting you? A dimensional shift that brings the same experience, although it is slightly different. Can you spot the differences? Most of the time, you can spot the changes in logos, in people, in spelling, or some other subtle variations. I'm pretty sure that you can at least relate to one of them. There's something bigger than us going on in here. Don't wake up in a different universe or dimension! It is not up to me!
I have a hunch that things are about to take a huge turn. I must head home. They are going to be perplexed.

II. Shapeshifters

Stephen has led the agency's scientific team graciously, making facts rule over theories. While Megan has brought a look of assurance and is soaking up pressure without succumbing to her peers' acumen and clever strategies. In fairness to Megan, she has dealt with misfortune and had to dodge particular attempts to close down her current research due to a lack of interest from the space agency. She was adamant about accepting praise for directing her efforts toward tangible results that no one can deny will benefit humanity. However, there's also been some backlash regarding deadlines and the practicality of her discoveries and inventions. They haven't backed off at all. Additionally, they intend to cut her funds and shut down some of the research she's been working on for over ten months, unless there's a huge breakthrough that convinces them that everything is worth the effort and resources. Given her brilliant approach, she has positioned herself in a tug of war with the agency that has given her some time to recover from her procrastination and lack of results.

Perhaps unsurprisingly, her standards have plummeted since she has diverted her efforts towards different projects. They have considered merging her project with Dr. Stanovic's exoplanet search. However, his reputation is chasing him and no female staff wants to work with him. I won't accept that!

At noon, Stephen comes to her laboratory and asks her, "Do you have a minute?" What for? I would like to share some notes on current research. Regarding what? It's about the speed of light. Okay, go ahead. I'm all ears. "You know that we cannot exceed the speed of light because that would surpass the velocity at which the system is loaded." What system? Don't play pretend, Megan. You are wrong, Steph. Why? We can exceed the speed of light. The only problem is that it won't be safe for humans. Special gear would be necessary to protect us from damage. We can still use it to send artificial intelligence or robots into deep space.

Here are the results of our most recent experiment, without any intention of debunking or refuting your premise. What are the findings? They are staggering. Why? A flash travels 310 times faster than the speed of light. Really? Yes. A pulse of light propagating at incredible speed is paradoxically detected at the exit of the cesium gas box, 1/62 billionth of a second before it enters. This is the result of a recent experiment conducted by Naim, which our own scientists say is astonishing.

Light in the form of packets or pulses can exceed 310 times that speed limit, which is 299,792,458 kilometers per second, under very specific conditions. This is because time and space form a whole, and the speed of information transmission is maximized in this whole. In addition to light, there exists a line between gravity, so to speak, action and reaction. This information is not going to be sent immediately due to confirmation and peer reviews required by the agency. Do you think there are other laws in the universe that are changing physics as we know it? Of course, we cannot be so arrogant as to think we know everything. This causes "strange things" depending on how fast one object moves relative to another. This includes an apparent increase in relativistic mass, a decrease in length, and a slowing of local time relative to measured time.

The simulation did not forbid exceeding the speed of light. Why do you need to? It is essential if you want to accomplish interstellar travel. You are obsessed with traveling to other galaxies, Stephen. Yes, indeed. If there is a universal speed limit that cannot be broken, it is because the system does not support those speeds, not because it affects people. If you can protect yourself with special equipment, that won't be the case anymore. What's all that nonsense? A video game cannot go faster than it needs to without damaging the processor or creating an increase in buffering because it messes up the perspective, visuals, and other decorative elements of the game. In our reality, it prevents us from reaching other parts of the universe. Someday, the right technology to vacation on other stars and meet potential inhabitants will be available. This is no longer a distant future goal, but a reality with star-shaped fusion reactors. It modifies the use of portals like "quantum tunnels" to allow shortcuts to other worlds. However, is it really like that? Although we don't want to ruin one of humanity's greatest dreams, is it possible the existence of portals that are safe for humans? How can we continue our journey beyond light without melting? The first question can only be answered if you use them.

For your last question, Megan, creating a protective bubble is the most viable option. So far, everything is going swimmingly. The most apprehensible functional problems are oxygen supply, gravity, radiation protection, and temperature control, among others.

An electron during quantum tunneling produces two photons more frequently than we think. Quantum two-photon communication of electrons is a current phenomenon, not a futuristic wonder of quantum physics. However, it is a potential guarantor of security in information technologies. Single light particles, the so-called photons, are used for secure data transmission and encryption. Can we somehow transfer humans as data? The discoveries of our physicists in solid-state research could be very useful in that regard. What results did you get, and what discovery do you refer to? The researchers found a light source that uses electron energy to produce a pair of photons. One of these light particles acts as a carrier of fragile quantum information, while the other can be used as a messenger to inform its sister particles. You still don't understand how this could help send humans to another dimension? It is currently difficult to assess whether the method of transmitting quantum information worked as planned. For instance, since quantum objects change states when they are observed or measured, if you send humans to another dimension, you won't know what happened to them until they return safely. In theory, can humans be digitized as data? Yeah, it's plausible in theory. However, I think it will be a sort of virtual avatar, right? All in all, it's like sending your memory and consciousness to another level in the universe. Do you need to forget about miniaturization for transportation to another dimension? Although I don't rule it out entirely, I prefer to explore other options as they allow me to reach unimaginable places without limits of time, food, oxygen, fuel, or other current physical limitations.

Quantum communication still has some drawbacks. It makes it difficult to control the information carried by photons. On the one hand, contact with the environment can destroy the quantum information carried by the photons; on the other hand, individual light particle sources often produce single photons at irregular intervals. So how can we know for sure when a photon is in progress without measuring it? Photon pairs can solve this problem. Photons act as messengers for their twins.

Researchers often use tunneling microscopes to probe the surface of conducting or semiconducting materials. The principle of such microscopes is based on the quantum tunneling effect. This indicates that electrons pass through the barrier with a certain probability. This is not usually accepted in classical physics. Forget about traditional science, once and for all. This is new science, a new perspective that has opened us a whole new world. You are right.

Furthermore, a voltage is applied from the metal tip and the electrons tunnel a short distance from the sample. Thus, light is produced when the electrons lose energy in this tunneling process. It is precisely this light that we have been investigating for several years. In addition to the individual light particles, the tunneling also produces photon pairs at frequencies 10,000 times higher than theory predicts. The probability of photon pair formation is theoretically so small that it should not normally be observed. However, our experiments show that photon pairs occur much more frequently. It was a big surprise for us. The physicists measured the photon pairs using two detectors that were used to determine the time interval between incident photons. At the moment when two photons pair up at the tunnel junction, the two photons are separated by less than 1/50 billionth of a second. It is not yet known whether the photons were produced simultaneously or in rapid succession. The resolution of the detector is not yet sufficient to transmit all the genetic information. Can humans be reconfigured on the other side of a quantum entanglement? That's the idea. Holly molly! What? That's mind-blowing!

I keep on thinking that we are inside something! What is that? A brain, perhaps. Nonsense, Steph! Maybe it is just a computer, a giant computer. What kind of computer? A quantum computer that keeps us prisoners of our own desires. You have no evidence to prove that. For instance, in a video game, you cannot see the whole world; you are just allowed to see the scene in which you are playing. Alright, keep on telling me. If you play faster than the game's loading speed, you will overcharge it and it will freeze or have patches. Are you telling me that our reality has some glitches? That's a possibility. I need to see to believe what you are telling me. I will find it and show it to you. That sounds fair to me, as long as you don't get crazy with the attempt. Sure, I won't. I think. It will make me steer the world with you. Dude, I've got you covered!

Alien transformation! What's that? It is the phenomenon in which an alien craft or being transforms into a completely terrestrial vehicle or individual in an astonishing and inexplicable manner. Perhaps the best known variant of this phenomenon today is the reptilian or metamorphic variant. Have you seen any? Yes, I have, and there are some cases that are exactly the same or even stranger.

Steph said, "I should be thinking about prioritizing research on the codes that Sydney is currently performing." Open and closed genetic codes may be boring. However, there's so much at stake that I cannot ignore it. It is better if I pitch in. What is hidden in Alien Transformation? In mythology, they are giant gods of the ancient earth. One of whom is the father of all. They are strange entities, described as a kind of semi-anthropomorphic demon compared to the divine beings of ancient Earth cultures. Before our eyes, they've spent so much time on our planet. Who? The shapeshifters! I really don't know who they are. To be honest with you, Stephen, this is the very first time I heard somebody talking about these beings. Welcome aboard!

The shapeshifters are adjusting the world to implement a new world order. A planet with a high temperature that matches their physiognomy and their needs. Do they really want to rule the earth? These humanoids rule the Earth and interfere at the highest levels of religious, economic, and political control with an absolute belief in being confused as humans. Do they think of banishing humans? They do not have to do that as long as they are in control of the situation and we do not seem to notice them, at least the way they really are. Is it on their agenda to change us? Yes, of course. They started a long time ago. How do they do it? They change our DNA. They are an endangered multidimensional species, and they will do whatever it takes to preserve their race. Even changing a race? They are not concerned about that. Where are they from? They probably come from Sirius B or Orion. They had colonies in both galaxies. Besides, they possess extensive knowledge of genetics, astronomy, and other fields of science, which is typical of such advanced civilizations. Were they confused with divine beings of the past? It was inevitable for a pre-civilization like ours that our ancestors took extraterrestrial beings for gods or angels. It is all over the world in cave art and geoglyphs in different cultures.

Dimensions are the vibratory levels in which different beings live, and shape-shifters live in the lower frequencies of the 4th and 5th dimensions that border the limits of the 3rd dimension, in which we humans live. We live in two dimensions, and we thought that the third dimension was just a misunderstanding of our reality. That's completely new territory for our scientific community. What do you mean? Other fields, such as esotericism, astrology, and others, have more knowledge about what is false or true regarding science. Paranormal or otherworldly? Yes, you heard it loud and clear.

What about "Superstring theory," also known as "M-theory?" It has allowed for the interesting hypothesis that the universe could have 10 or 11 dimensions, 10 of which are spatial and one temporal. Are you sure that it is just a hypothesis? It is our turn to prove it right or wrong. What a challenge! Furthermore, seven of those dimensions are invisible to our eyes and current technology because they trigger invisible gravitational waves. That explains many phenomena that have puzzled science for a long time. Electromagnetic waves can travel between these extra dimensions, extending cosmic space beyond the classical four dimensions.

There are parallel universes in which you don't want to get trapped. Why? Their strangeness will scare the hell out of you. Is it possible for realities other than our own to exist? That's one of the challenges of science in general and physics in particular. The goal is to prove that such a hypothesis is possible and to find a way to travel between universes. There is a theoretical proposal in physics that works only if the universe is multidimensional. However, if you take paranormal, spiritual, etheric, divine, etc. dimensions, you reach up to 30 dimensions. They have no scientific basis, though. It's not the way we do science. The fact that they cannot be explained does not justify disqualifying or dismissing them. It is a valid point. Congratulations, we agree on something. Of course, you are a staunch Stephen because you always accept the weirdest phenomena as common and feasible. How well do you understand them? Not so much if you fooled me a couple of times. What? You thought I didn't notice those affairs. I was just pretending to be stupid. Thus, I didn't suffer your testosterone attacks. You should have known better. What's more, everything has its limits, and that science lesson was the last straw for me. Who? Please don't play pretend. I try to get along with you at work out of courtesy and because sometimes we have some activities in common. I have no choice but to put up with you sporadically. The greatness of your work masks the stupidity of the hormones you act on. What do you mean? You're not a child anymore, you're a grown man, and you don't act like that. They love their job more than anything in the world. You will forget about your family and stay in the laboratory for days. You are right, I am very selfish with my needs and priorities. Someone knocks on the door and interrupts her. It's Emmett. I know you're busy. However, thank you for your time. What's up, Emmett? There's a lot of euphoric activity in the area. I thought you might want to take a look around. Really? Of course, I didn't spend time just saying hello. All the scientists were called into the main room. There are many authorities on the subject from other countries to analyze what is going on. We will continue this conversation at another time. not interested.

Your colleague talks about science showing that "parallel dimensions" such as the universe are part of the so-called multiverse. This is a hypothetical set of multiple possible universes, including our own, that together make up all of reality. Does that include simulations and baby universes created by other beings? This includes the millions of universes created, simulations and other worlds that escape the realm of reality, ghostly, spiritual. It is possible to fall into the physical, etheric, and paranormal.

What would it be like to travel between dimensions? We are already answering that question with one of our projects. Amazing!

By the way, we were talking about shapeshifters before, and we didn't conclude our topic due to all the hype around us. What else can I tell you? Whatever you want. Everything is new to me. Listen, they have the ability to perform incredible transformations, assuming a completely human form, entering our dimension and dominating us. How did they get here? A kind of interdimensional vortex seems to be generated through the wormhole. Due to the origin of certain situations, we can see a completely random pattern of events. This is how we gain comforting beliefs through the explanation of the unknown, however crazy it may be. Do they have something to do with the simulation? I don't know yet. They are very secretive, which encourages the desire to hide something. The paradox of knowledge and its sources of access has been revealed. If it is the "Transmuters" who live among us and have secret plans, why don't they come forward and reveal their plans? They will provide us with information that will take us to another level of civilization in the universe.

Is all the information you provide us with reliable? It is denied by the elite-controlled official hegemonic science, which dismisses shapeshifters as violent or dangerous. Current and future information management is important here. We all know that our reality in cyberspace is evolving more and more every day. Based on this, as we know, virtualization is gaining ground over reality. Audiovisual stimulation as a means of transmitting information is immense. Virtual reality will allow you to literally feel, not just hear and see. It will be the ultimate triumph of simulation. Being in the rough terrain of simulation can be unnerving and, at times, dangerous. Anyone who challenges it disappears, and there are many examples of scientists remaining silent in one way or another. Not at all. This is bigger than us.

While Emmett was driving along a lonely, deserted road, he saw two women on the road. These women were heading eastbound on his route, and he pulled over to the side of the road to ask about the accident. They were fine and had no cars. How did you get to such a remote place? They didn't say a word. She thought it was some kind of trauma and helped him into the car. He aimed his car lights at only a few rocks and three unidentified circular objects, emitting a constant bright flashing light. Another corpse hovered a few feet off the ground. Suddenly, these objects turned into a triangular craft, and the hovering woman boarded the craft and disappeared at high speed. At the same time, I was surprised. I was interested in what their eyes saw, I was trying to get an answer from the passengers. They stared at me and walked down the street. A few miles later, the spacecraft flew over the SUV several times. One of the

women who appeared to be injured when I picked her up had already fully recovered. To my surprise. They both responded in unison. We are Kat121 and Kat122. What an interesting name you have. Are you kidding me? They looked at each other, then I stopped. The frightened girls jumped aboard and sped away. I continued my journey, dazed and unable to comprehend what had happened. Nobody will believe me.
After a few hours, the lights of the spaceship brought me to my senses. They are following me. What for? I will manage to distance myself from it, entering a tunnel that will finally lead me to the city. Later, I entered a large building and continued to the underground parking lot. However, as I exited the vehicle towards the elevators, I saw three small lights above my head, about the size of a headlamp, which I thought at the moment were some other cars' beams. And I breathed a sigh of relief. Suddenly, the lights began to rise and move erratically. I stood motionless over the cargo area. The lights rushed towards me again. I must get away while I can. As I rush into the elevator, the lights accompany me all the time. Who are they? You know us, Kat... It's you! Yes! Where are you from? What do you want from me? We've come a long way, and we won't hurt you. I was paralyzed, as if a force had taken hold of me. I can't move. Why are you doing this to me? The lights flew out of the building, through the walls. And I collapsed onto the floor. A security guard came to my rescue. Is it something wrong, sir? No, thank you. I think I tripped. The floor seems to be slippery with the rain. However, it was not raining. The man was stumped and saw me walk away towards my vehicle.

Disconcerted and scared to death, he arrives at his office where he records an account of what happened to pass the report to his immediate superior. When he finally sent it, there was an order to take all the videos from the surveillance cameras. The women were seen to appear and turn into light and then into the ship. What was that all about, Emmett? If I could explain it, I wouldn't have asked for your help. Several planes were sent to the area in search of the ship. Are they crazy? Do they think they're going to reach that alien ship in those obsolete planes? They are hypersonic, and we have nothing better. Triangular UFOs were seen flying on the other side of the world. There is no way we can intercept them.

Even though the nightmare was not over yet. I arrived home very late that night. I was again contacted by the alien visitors. They appeared in front of me. This time, I calmed down and spoke slowly. I made sure my camera was recording everything and then I dialed the agency's number for backup. The ladies repeated in chorus, "We want to help you." With what? With your planet. You have to talk to somebody else. I have neither the authority nor the power to do what you want. Can you take us to your leader? Sure, I can.

A dark shadow approached with incandescent green eyes and jumped down next to Emmett. It's my pet! That's my cat. Don't be afraid of him. The young girls looked at the animal curiously. Don't you have animals on your planet? In the silence of the night, a distant thud caught their attention, and a group of lights appeared on the horizon. The noise grew louder and louder, and suddenly, the lights lit up the room. A small army had arrived to support Emmett. The ladies, transforming into light, came out onto the

agents. Before their eyes they became a gigantic spaceship. And a powerful blue light blinded them. The street was full of spectators. There were dozens, maybe hundreds. And in a moment, everything was gone. The cars and the agents left the scene. Emmett stayed on the couch with his cat, "Lucky." The lights went out and the television came on. And a dim light came through the walls. Then he realized they hadn't gotten away. They continued on with him.
He decides to take them to visit his friend and scientist, Sydney. He wasn't tired at all, even after a sleepless night. He calls Sydney and tells her he has some friends who want to meet her. I will be there in five minutes! Upon arrival, Emmett rings the bell. Sydney is looking through her video-intercom, and she is scared at what she sees. No, no, I can't believe my eyes. She manages to open the door. Who did you bring with you, Emmett? You will find out about it later. My friends are not of this world. It is too late to go to the laboratory, and that would be suspicious and would raise some red flags in the security area. That's true. We've got to go to the laboratory. Not now, it's 3:11 a.m. Are you crazy, Emmett? I know that would be chaos for base security. Absolutely! What do you suggest then? Stay here for a couple of hours, and then we can depart to our destination. The morning shift usually starts at 6:00 a.m. That sounds good to me. Emmett hugs Sydney. She said, "What?" Night. Where are the aliens going to stay? They will be fine in their spacecraft and will join us in the morning. You can stay over there on the sofa, Emmett. I thought that you would offer me a bed. I only have one. Don't press your luck. He laughed and replied, "That's fine with me." You'd better.   She brought him some

blankets. As he watched her walk, Emmett sighed. I hadn't noticed how beautiful she is!

At sunrise, Sydney woke Emmett up; it's time to hit the road, young man. Oh gosh! I fell deeply asleep. Come on! They were talking on the way to the laboratory when they noticed something unusual had happened. Everything looks different! The railings on the road were different, the signs, and the whole environment was different. When we arrived at the laboratory, the parking lot was open. They walked in together, and Sydney greeted them, then she said, "Who are you?" The girls turned into dancing lights. She repeated, "Who are you?" Haven't you noticed? I found them on the side of the road while visiting my family on the East Highway. Where's their spacecraft? All I can tell you is that every time they panic, it picks them up, or shall I say, they turn into a spacecraft! What? Yes, exactly like that, my darling.

Why did you bring them to me? So they can tell us what they want. They said they wanted to help us. For what? You told me about the planet. Emmett, we're not worthy of a situation of this magnitude. I know. However, before you talk to the directors and presidents of the agencies, you should know what they're talking about and if they can really be trusted. I want to know If they wanted to, they would have done it by now. I do. However, I am always a skeptic and take things very seriously. You never know what to expect from otherworldly beings.

Let's talk to them. Show us your true self. They looked around their surroundings. Then, it all started. They witnessed another event of a singular nature. Three strange and gigantic faceless beings lay down on the floor of the laboratory. And in a matter of seconds, after exchanging a small blue sphere, they got up and walked towards the computers, where they transformed into light and back to a human form, dressed in regular clothes. Shapeshifters! What? These beings are "metamorphs" that can change their shape at will. Like chameleons? No, not really. They just change their color, while these shapeshifters are more extreme. What do they look like? A universe of options. Yes, that's true. Endless possibilities. Shapeshifting gives them the super ability to be almost everything. Where do you think we can find this species? Here on earth, we have some octopus at the bottom of the sea. Yeah, right. Seriously, in all cultures, you have some reference to such beings who undergo such transformations, from animals to deities. What could they be in space? They could be anything, like plants, animals, or the universe itself! How come? They could turn into stars, planets, or something else. We are just speculating. Those elusive creatures have some invisible abilities and disguise themselves as objects or the environment, such as dark matter and dark energy, which are invisible to human eyes.

Take us to your leader. We will. Emmett contacted the agency director, who promised to tell the president. A secret meeting was agreed. The president has a very tight schedule. However, due to the unprecedented nature of these visitors, he will join us in a couple of hours. Knock it off, Chief Andrews! We know that's part of your rhetoric. This is the greatest single event in the history of aerospace and the search for extraterrestrial intelligence. We are not talking about collecting stones in some strange space spot or a phony prank; this is the real deal. We know and we value your loyalty. Mr. Andrews contacted the aeronautical and space leaders to be part of the secret meeting.

Upon arrival, the president was conducted to a conference room, and minutes later, our visitors were received. The president managed to ask, "Can I see you the way you are?" Kat121 responded, "You are always asking us to show you our real appearance." As they did several transformations back and forth, they were all in shock. "This is beyond words," said Mr. Andrews. We've spent a lifetime waiting for this moment, and now suddenly we are in front of these beings. Let's get into business. What is it that you want from us? We are here to help you. With what? Your planet must be protected from evil. What can you do for our planet? We can provide you with the knowledge to take it to a level you have never imagined. Are you talking about alien technology? We are all aliens. No, we are humans! Humans don't belong here either. You are the child of the stars too. I see. What do we need to do to receive your gift? Use it wisely, is all we are going to ask. You can count on it. Humans! You will soon need to defend your world from unimaginable creatures and threats. Can you help us fight against them? We do not fight or kill, and you shouldn't do that either. What are we going to do then? You will have the power in your hands.

Now, we are going to work with your scientists. Sure, proceed. Mr. Andrews and Dr. Faith will join Sydney and Emmett. The president and his entourage departed quickly and with a smirk on their faces.

The scientist cohort quietly followed the alien friends, playing alongside. Are there any other species of aliens on Earth? Yes, there are currently three species living permanently on your planet. Who are they? Besides the "Repts," who are human like and are almost everywhere, you have the mole people who live underground, and there's another population of amphibian beings living in the depths of the sea. They used to be some others in the past. When? By the time we arrived for the first time on your planet, there were some grays and some "Avlastians." What happened to them? The latter were forced to leave since they were barbarians. Regarding the advanced civilizations, they are just monitoring from afar. They are the observers of the cosmos. They don't intend, by any means, to come and live with you. What about you? We had no choice but to wander around the universe, helping endangered civilizations like yours. Are you going to stay? No, we cannot. We have to go to some other places. You are going to be on your own.

They started using the computers soon after they were overheated due to an extremely heavy work overload. Mr. Andrews and Dr. Faith have been recoding everything. Nothing is left to their memory. Sydney suggested using a large quantum computer that's at the back of her office. That seemed to be a perfect fit for their visitors. After a while, the visitors give Sydney a crystal. She asked them, "What is this?" This is the most valuable knowledge in the cosmos. "Is that classified knowledge?" Mr. Andrews asked. Sydney said, "Shut up! This is not the time for such foolish procedures. " Dr. Faith agreed and got closer to see in detail what was there. Mr. Andrews wanted to check if there were any far-fetched weapons. Kat123 said, "You are now the guardian of the code." What code? The code of codes that holds the secrets of the cosmos Is it contained in the crystal? It has what you need to access the database of the universe. Bear in mind that the most valuable information lies within you. The visitors turned into light and then a triangle spacecraft. In front of our eyes, they vanished into the horizon.

Mr. Andrews posted guards outside the base complex, and there was a small army surrounding the premises of the laboratory. Military experts came to join the scientific group. A joint effort toward a common goal.

Touching the crystal, Sydney reads some cryptic riddles. Oh no! What's wrong with you? They left us more decoding to get to the secrets. Subatomic particles down the rabbit hole, some tetraquarks and pentaquarks, are moving oddly. They show us new ways of reality with exotic structures.

Stephen got the news that some scientists claim they have encountered glitches. Wait a minute! Where? They are all over the world. There are some signs of a simulated reality, the one in which we live. Can you be more specific? Yes, indeed. I experienced that sensation once. What was that? I went back to the university where I did my undergraduate studies to take some random courses, and most of the things were different. In which ways? Although some old buildings were still standing in the same places. They have certainly built others around them. That usually happens over a long time. Thus, that's nothing weird. It was definitely not the same. How could things be so different? It seems that it was another dimension. This is a science asylum! Not really.

We have some monumentally stupid people around us. Who are those? Some dumb politicians who prefer lies over science. You know that facts will always win, and the truth comes out triumphant. Not always!

Mr. Andrews let the president know of the latest developments at the base. He said, "We have the secret code, sir." What the heck is that? It grants us all the knowledge that we need to become a super civilization. Does that include alien technology and weapons? Yes, sir. It includes everything. Don't waste time and begin to manufacture everything. We are already working on that. However, we need funds to accomplish such a gargantuan task. Sure, I will give a speech tomorrow at the congress and later at the general assembly, so the world will have our leadership during these tumultuous times. Keep me posted. Yes, sir.

Stephen is pondering the possibility of an invisibility cloak, some sort of device that hides them. There's a story of a kraken-like alien creature that lurks in the depths of space, in voids and darkness, destroying planets, galaxies, and even universes. Who told you that? It was revealed to me in a dream. That was a nightmare, Megan. Whatever! Sydney thinks this is a premonition. "Airawnk" was clear in mind. I still see it as a gigantic squid, covering galaxies and even bigger. You are foreseeing the future as dark as it may come to us. You should remind yourself that the past, present, and future are all the same, in one timeline. It is only our perception that makes them different.

The president begins his speech with, "A herculean effort carried out by our scientists along with our military has brought the cooperation of an alien race that has uninterestedly donated their knowledge to help us face this crisis the world is undergoing." Science is our bedrock, and under my guidance, we won't perish. Let me address some unfounded remarks that are pure conspiracy and unfairly attribute to our country a selfish position. This is the first time I've been irritated. Our visitors will be back tomorrow to greet the world and witness the new order that has just begun!

III. Symmetrons

Where's Stephen? He took a couple of days off. What about Sydney? She hasn't shown up today. That's very unusual. Is there anything wrong with her? You should ask her. I don't have anything else to tell you. Don't be rude! I'm just being honest, Megan. She barely notices me and sometimes greets me with a fake smile. Oh, that's pretty much her. Don't feel bad; she's like that most of the time. Her mind is always wandering around in some special dimension. I guess you are right.
Stephen is on his way to a hiking trail to refresh his mind. For me, it's not just a sporting activity, it's contact with the environment. Starting at the base of the mountain, I buckled up and checked my pack and gear. There are only about 6,000 steps and platform areas, cable segments that require suspension, and vertical ladders to traverse all the way to the top of the mountain. There is a forest on the side of the road, distracting you for a few seconds while you admire the beautiful scenery and panorama in all directions. At the same time, I enjoy the practical perspective of moving my body in the fresh air of nature. I'm not competing with anyone here. You are competing only with yourself in endurance. You don't have to push your body to the limit. It relaxes my mind and leaves all work stress and personal problems behind for at least a few hours. It's a great activity to enjoy happily

with the regulars on the route and the occasional stranger. We always share wonderful moments and experiences and get away from the routine. There were a lot of people in line today, so we waited about 3 hours before the hiking started. I still have a long way to go, so I want to forget about time and enjoy the journey.

The scenery over there is just amazing, even though this is the most dangerous mountain trail in the world. That's crazy, people! Yes, I would be terrible when it comes to communicating with the guides as I don't speak their language. There you are! The front line of life!

It's shocking. This is a two-way staircase to heaven. When you go up, people will come down, and you have to avoid or cross them at a certain point to escape. People with a fear of heights should never look down. Not me, so I'm enjoying the scenery. However, you may feel dizzy.

This is one of the most dangerous challenges. The breathtaking hike takes you literally to the sky. The instructor is explaining to us how the harness works. Basically, you hold two carabiners attached to ropes. On descent, the carabiners must be individually released and reattached under each hook on the hillside. If you accidentally unclip both carabiners at once, it's game over. I'd better be careful.

Unlike other typical mountains with one central dominating peak, this one is spread out into five peaks: South Peak, North Peak, East Peak, West Peak, and Central Peak. The North Peak is located alone in the northern part of the whole scenic area, and the other four peaks are located all together in the south, only a few hundred meters from each other. Some of these peaks are over 2,000 meters high.

To finish a hike on the mountain in a single day, you'd better get to the tourist center at the foot of the mountain in the early morning before crowds show up, or you will have to wait in long lines to purchase tickets. I do not recommend this insanity. You should give yourself more time to fully enjoy the hike without any rush.

I will be able to hike all the walking trails on the mountain and have opportunities to enjoy the precious sunset and sunrise. However, it may be a huge pressure on my feet and knees, and some sections of the trails have to be walked twice. To protect my knees and avoid walking repeated trails, I was advised to start hiking up the mountain from the temple. You must climb with full concentration and hold the iron chains tight. It takes approximately a couple of hours to get to the North Peak. I'm taking a break for sightseeing and resting a bit. Then we will leave, either for another peak or down the mountain. It all depends on how we feel and the level of energy we still have available. People may spend more time queuing up in the lines trying to get down the plank road than anything else. That's why I started very early.

It is said to be one of the most dangerous hiking trails in the world. The plank road was constructed on the surface of a vertical cliff. Iron stakes are nailed into the cliff, and wire ropes link the stakes together. Narrow planks are placed on the stakes for you to move steps. Above the plank road, there are another two lines of wire rope fixed on the surface of the cliff. You can move steps while holding the safety rope.

I saw local people chugging up the mountain paths like it was nothing. This mountain is a sacred place. It feels holy.
At the Near East Peak, we met the second on the "Heaven's Ladder." This was much higher and steeper than the first "Stairway to Heaven." I was carrying a heavy rucksack, so I was sure I would fall. By the time I got to his last third, my palms were very sweaty, even in very cold temperatures. That's cold sweat. Along the summit near East His Peak is a fence adorned with gold locks and red ribbons. It is customary for visitors to purchase locks on the mountain and attach them to iron chains to pray for the health and safety of their friends and family. At least the ground is below you if you go down. The stairs are carved into the wall. You can imagine hikers in an era when tourist infrastructure used only steps and they didn't have to wrestle with harnesses or cables.
Still, it was nice to have all the safety equipment. When I turned around, there were only clouds. I could see low peaks in the distance. For a moment, the clouds that had lingered all day began to clear, and I was able to catch a glimpse of the landscape below. The climb is fairly straight. I slipped a few times. If I hadn't been tied down, I probably would have fallen about 20 feet. The safety instructor at the top told us not to bring cameras, but come on. Today, it is a must to have photos and videos. Most people documented the transition. However, once you reach the bottom of the cliff, the fear eases a little. There are carved rock steps leading to the top. At the end of the path, there is a pavilion with a chessboard. Some say it's the tallest chessboard in the world. As the sun rises over

East Peak, you can imagine two monks competing on a chessboard. I have a smile on my face. Nevertheless, I was panicking the whole time. I was sure there was no way I would come back until the last group collapsed. On second thought, I really wanted to stay in the mountains, which I was really excited about. After a quick soak in the moment at the chess pavilion, I left everyone behind and ran up the cliff face. It was a bit silly to be honest. At one point, I didn't even bother to clip the carabiner. If you didn't have a safety rope, don't tell my mother that you almost fell. From there, we sprinted to get back to North Peak in time for the cable car. I was basically about to do a two-hour hike up and down in approximately 40 minutes. I may have missed the plank walk, even though it certainly turned the hike into "the most exciting and dangerous hike on the planet."

At the base of Central Peak, the fog cleared completely for the first time that day. **It was a stunning sight.** However, I didn't have time to enjoy it.

Camping is allowed on the mount. However, you should not camp in the forest area or on the cliff side of the mountain; not hinder the paths; not punch holes in the constructed area or near tourist facilities; and not use fireworks during camping. I ended up camping for the cold night and will begin my descent early the next morning. I was not the only one there. I saw maybe ten others staying around. While waiting to get down the mountain, I met two swimmers from my hometown who had traveled to go only to do the "plank walk" after seeing the videos online. Two other guys, with a background in the military, joined us too. Then we sprinted to get to the hiking path off the "plank walk," and made it slowly and at a painstaking pace to the base of the mountain. It was a good thing I didn't try to push my luck going to the other side of the mountain. I would never have made it. We started at sunrise and got down at noon, almost ready for lunch.

Stephen waved the group goodbye. They agreed to get together some other time in the future for a different experience. When my co-workers see the video of me doing this, they will go nuts!

Mr. Andrews said, "Those appalling cowards must have killed Naim." We're all aghast at this unexpected disappearance. They went too far.

Back at work after the exhilarating hike, Stephen was deep in his thoughts and didn't perceive the presence of Megan behind him. He's saying to himself, "Invisible walls between galaxies, "symmetrons" and an unknown fifth force." What is going on in the universe? Oh, that's you, Megan. Yes, who else are you expecting? Nobody else. I know you are in another world, far from our reality. You can say so.

How could our ancestors understand the nature of the cosmos even more insightfully than what science is reaching today? That's a tough question, my dear. Cosmologists have been grappling with a unique problem for years. Something that, in the light of current theories, simply does not make sense. What's that, if you don't mind my asking? They are the small satellite galaxies orbiting the Milky Way and other neighboring galaxies, such as Andromeda or Centaurus A. What exactly are you worried about? They are incomprehensibly "synchronized," all lined up and forming thin flat disks, like Saturn's rings, instead of being distributed in disordered orbits around our galaxy, as predicted by the standard model of cosmology. Yes, the so-called "Lambda Cold Dark Matter model' (ΛCDM)." Yes, that's right. The theory that astronomers use to understand the universe we live in. Did you know that our universe has invisible walls that act as boundaries between galaxies? No, I thought that scientists' proposals just filled the voids of theoretical constructs without any practicality. Far from glamorous, my dear. You live and learn, darling.

Astrophysicists suspect that a "fifth force," mediated by a hypothetical particle called a "symmetron," may be at work in space. Where can we find it? We don't even know if it exists. Yes, it does. The research points to a first potential explanation of "new physics" that does not completely eliminate dark matter. Please tell me. Some agitated people shouting outside the laboratory distracted them. Something is wrong. There's too much noise outside. We'd better check what's going on in the base.

The Lambda Cold Dark Matter Model (ΛCDM) is the current standard model for explaining cosmology and understanding the universe. However, this model had a mysterious challenge that contradicted its predictions. To explain what seems like nonsense, scientists have now proposed the existence of a new "fifth force" that may be at work in outer space. Do you agree with that? That doesn't matter at all. Researchers suggest that small galaxies may accommodate the invisible "wall" of a new virtual class of particles called "Symmetrons." We are trying to fill this gap with a proposal that may rewrite the laws of astrophysics. A "Fifth force!"

Do you have any details on this new theory? Enough to know that something doesn't fit. Why not? There's something missing. That's what I am working on right now.

The standard ΛCDM theory suggests that the universe is composed of three key elements. The cosmological constant supports the general theory of relativity; the cold dark matter that moves slowly through the universe without radiation; and the general matter that we interact with every day. That theory implies that smaller galaxies should be attracted by the gravity of larger host galaxies. This would make their orbits erratic. However, our fellow scientists have not been able to verify this in the real world. To solve this curious gap between theory and observation, known as the "satellite disk problem" or the "satellite plane problem," scientists have proposed many possible explanations that seem unlikely to be true.

Now, researchers may have come up with a better explanation. As they propose, the "fifth force" could guide these small "satellite" galaxies, as astronomers often call them, into strange orbits around the larger galaxies, ending up arranged in thin planes, or disks, almost like Saturn's rings. Yeah, right. They presented what they believe is "the first potential 'new physics' explanation for the observed satellite planes that does not dispense with dark matter," referring to the unidentified substance that makes up most of the mass of the universe. Symmetrons could explain dark matter, don't you think? What about photons, Higgs bosons, tachyons, and other subatomic particles? You are taking us down to the microscopic world. Yes, indeed, straight to the quantum-verse.

This is too speculative to be taken as a serious theory to create a new Physics. What do you suggest, then? Symmetrons, which researchers have used to explain gaps in our knowledge of the cosmos, could generate this "force" to form "domain walls," or boundaries in space, while explaining dark matter. We know we need new particles because we have dark matter and dark energy. Therefore we suspect we're going to need to add new particles to our standard model to account for those things. That's exactly what you are doing. Although the theory is still being worked out, it could explain small galaxies developing disks around larger host galaxies, as seen in these synchronized orbits around our own galaxy, the Milky Way, as well as its nearest galactic neighbors, Andromeda and Centaurus A. Symmetrons could exist in clusters of "different polar states," in turn forming invisible walls around them. What about plasma? That's what most of us expected them to be made of. Their claim that there is a 50% chance that different regions will use different values for their symmetries is still speculative. This could explain the differences that some larger galaxies exhibit in the most densely populated galaxies but not anywhere else. This could explain the differences that some larger galaxies show in the smaller galaxies that orbit them. This theory needs to be tested, and I don't think it will stand the test.

As interesting as the new theory may be, many questions remain unanswered. Here comes my colleague Naim. We have a lot of work ahead of us to prove them wrong. I don't want to throw dirt on their research. We are working with science. We don't do that. If we decide to prove the existence of such invisible walls in space, we would have to prove that symmetrons exist too. Perhaps looking at some of the early universe with a powerful telescope will tell us more about these new particles and the organization they bring to the universe. Particle colliders are also a good attempt to find clues on how to proceed with this research. That's a great suggestion, Naim.

The "Fifth force" forms an invisible wall in the universe, separating galaxies. Megan said, "That's an indication of what we talked about earlier, Stephen." Yes, it may be. Naim asked, "What was that?" Some glitches in reality. Are you talking about simulation? They all laughed.

Current research has pointed out a "fifth force" that may be at work in space. However, it failed to resolve some observations that did not agree with its rationale, even adjusting for these differences, suggesting that smaller galaxies may fit these "walls" created by a new virtual class of particles called Symmetrons. These symmetrons may create "domain walls" or "forces" that form boundaries in space, explaining dark matter by referring to the unidentified matter that makes up most of the mass of the universe. We have discussed that prior to your arrival, Naim. There was endless talk in the agency about the risk of unfulfilled potential already. There's so much at stake, we should be perfectionists if we want to continue our research, or they will cut our funds. Tension is nothing new to us. Even amidst all of that we delivered, they required us to achieve one of the greatest ever discoveries. Some people look at you, Stephen, as a snub, sometimes kind of arrogant. Megan interrupted, "What the heck! Leave him alone!"

The wall is covered in galaxy spatter. What's that? Wrong question, my friend. You should have asked, "Who's that?" Or shall I say, where is that? Any answer is welcome at this moment. Stephen's unwavering pursuit of perfection is relentless.

Regarding the presence of symmetrons, these particles exist in groups of "different polar states" and can form an invisible wall around them. The key point is how to detect such elusive particles. That's when we step in and find ways to achieve such a feat. It became clear to Naim that they were not playing any games; they were going for all or nothing.

According to the researchers, there is a 50% chance that different parts of the universe have different values due to symmetry. This will explain the difference between several large galaxies and the smaller galaxies orbiting them. We are embroiled in a race for excellence, pursuing these unknown particles with a course of unfortunate events that is plausible and easily foreseeable. Sydney added, "There's something I've learned during my time with this team; we will never give up, and Steph always makes someone's talent stand out." He's enthralled, as everyone else is, by the soaking conditions of the laboratory. This is unbearably hot. We turned off the air conditioner to achieve better results at room temperature. It's muggy all over.

How can we prove that Symmetrons are real? We don't have to prove anything. We'll find out about them and we'll take it from there. What do you mean? If they don't exist, then we have to find an alternative explanation. What if they do exist? That's a solid case for a detailed study.

The first measurements of dark matter since nearly the beginning of the universe are finally complete. Scientists combined massive samples of distant galaxies with lensing distortions to discover even older dark matter. Those scientists studied the properties of dark matter surrounding galaxies that emerged 12 billion years ago. These results offer the intriguing possibility that the fundamental rules of cosmology differ when we examine the early history of our universe. Because the speed of light is limited, distant galaxies appeared billions of years ago rather than today, with the exception of dark matter, which does not emit light and is therefore even more difficult to observe.

As predicted by general relativity, in more distant source galaxies, farther than those in which dark matter is studied, their gravitational attraction on the dark matter-bearing source galaxies distorts the surrounding space-time When the light from the original galaxy passes through this distortion, it bends and changes the apparent shape of the galaxy. As dark matter increases, the same effect has altering the surrounding. This allowed scientists to apply this distortion to degree the quantity of darkish depend surrounding the foreground galaxy. Nevertheless, at some point, scientists run into problems. Galaxies in the deepest part of the universe are incredibly dark. Therefore, the farther away from Earth, the less effective this technique will be. Lensing distortion is often subtle and difficult to notice, so many background galaxies are required to see the signal. Most previous studies adhere to the same limits. They could not detect the source galaxy far enough away to measure the distortion, and they could only analyze dark matter only 8 to 10 billion years old. These limitations leave open the question of how the dark matter was distributed between this point and the beginning of the universe, 13.7 billion years ago.

To overcome these problems and observe dark matter in the distant universe, our research team used another source of background light, microwaves, emitted by the Big Bang itself. First, using observational data from the survey, the team identified 1.5 million visible-light lenticular galaxies that were selected for observation 12 billion years ago. It then uses microwaves from the cosmic microwave background, the leftover radiation from the Big Bang, to overcome the lack of light from even more distant galaxies. Using satellite-observed microwaves, the team measured how dark matter around the target galaxy distorted the microwaves.

Trying to see dark matter around distant galaxies was "a crazy idea." Using massive samples of distant galaxies and lensing distortions, we found that dark matter goes back 12 billion years. Since that was only 1.7 billion years after the beginning of the universe, these galaxies can be seen soon after they formed. I opened a new window this time. Twelve billion years ago, the situation was very different. More galaxies are seen in the process of forming than now. The first galaxy clusters are also beginning to form. A galaxy cluster contains between 100 and 1000 galaxies and is held together gravitationally by a large amount of dark matter. The results not only provide a very consistent picture of galaxies and their evolution, but also of the dark matter in and around galaxies and how this picture evolves over time.

One of the most interesting findings concerns the aggregation of dark matter. Going back in time, the standard model is flawed. If the results hold after reducing the uncertainty, this is exciting because it could suggest improvements in models that could provide information about the nature of dark matter itself. As we can see in the resulting images, from asteroids close to our solar system to the most distant galaxies in the early universe, many new questions can be explored using the same data.

Pseudo-quantum telepathy experiments suggest that reality does not exist until it is measured. Stephen successfully used quantum telepathy and entangled quantum particles to test simulation theory and push the boundaries of probability and classical statistics. We've been wrong for a long time; reality may be more fragile than we expected it to be. Using "quantum pseudo-telepathy," a sort of trick where reality is elusive and seems to be real when it is systematically weighed, as quantum physics explains, things are not always there unless you see them.

To illustrate this point, our team of physicists developed a series of theoretical combination games that have limited chances of winning unless the two players can communicate with each other. However, if measurement is limited to revealing actual existence, this can be systematically conquered using pseudo-quantum telepathy. In other words, both players can always win by taking advantage of quantum effects.

Is this a wave-particle duality? The idea that a physical object can exist in two mutually exclusive states at the same time is also known as wave-particle duality. For example, photons can be polarized such that the electric field they contain rotates vertically, horizontally, or in both directions simultaneously, at least until it is measured. At this point, the bidirectional state is reduced to random vertically or horizontally. More importantly, no matter how the bidirectional state collapses, the observer cannot assume that the measurements only indicate how polarized the photons already are. Polarization only appears during the measurement. What about quantum entanglement? So, two photons can be highly entangled, each in an uncertain state in either direction. However, their polarizations are highly correlated, so that if one is horizontal, the other must be vertical and vice versa. The ability to extract concrete reality from the quantum ether in this way opens up the possibility of overcoming the limitations of classical statistics. For games, players equipped with certain quantum resources can perform better than those equipped with classical ones. To test their claim, the team of physicists used a Magic Square game experiment, in which two players "colluded" to measure photons. The fictitious players named Aria and Brian measure photons individually and plot the results as "1" or "-1" on a 3x3 grid. After recording the values, a virtual judge arrives and randomly selects one of Aria's rows and one of Brian's columns. If both players have the same number of overlapping fields, they win. The rules require "parity" to prevent Aria and Brian from rigging the game by agreeing to put the same number in each box. That is, all entries in Aria's row are multiplied by 1, and Brian's column is multiplied by 1 to -1. Most importantly, two players cannot talk to each other during the game. Is it statistically impossible to win all the time? If such a game were played in the real world, the 9-square grids of the two players would have to differ by at least 1 square. In other words, it is statistically impossible to win more than 8 times in 9 rounds. However, in the quantum world, Aria and Brian can always win. This is because quantum mechanics eliminates the need to put a fixed value in each square before the round takes place, so only a "1" or a "-1" will appear if the referee makes a decision. Therefore, interleaving ensures that the numbers in the key cells match and that the measurements also follow the parity rules.

In other words, the whole scheme works because the values arise only when the measurements are made: the measurements are actually causing the results, not the other way around. The rest of the grid is irrelevant since the values do not exist for the measurements that Aria and Brian never make.

Does the winning percentage beat the classic statistic? A game like that can't be a theoretical exercise. Nevertheless, it can be demonstrated using entangled quantum particles. To do this, the experimenters used an ultrafast laser pulse to excite a barium borate crystal, producing pairs of subparticles, specifically photons that are entangled in two directions. More specifically, the photons were entangled in such a way that the polarization of one was intrinsically linked to the orbital angular momentum of the other, which determines whether a wavy photon is shifted to the right or to the left. Using these values as surrogates for the player numbers, Aria and Brian won 93.84% of 1,075,930 rounds, beating the maximum of 88.89% with hidden variables. Although not perfect, the 93.84% winning percentage exceeds what should be possible according to classical statistics, proving that physical reality is not fixed and can be manipulated through quantum entanglement. Quantum advantage through "pseudotelepathy." A "reality" difficult to digest? Or would it be better to say a simulation is difficult to believe?

In other words, the whole scheme works because values occur only when measurements are taken. Measurements actually generate results, not the other way around. The rest of the grid is irrelevant because there are no measurements that Aria and Brian don't make. Do their win rates exceed traditional statistics? A game like this cannot be done with paper and ink. However, it can be demonstrated with entangled quantum particles. To do this, the experimenters used an ultrafast laser pulse to excite a barium borate crystal, producing pairs of photons that entangle in two directions. More specifically, the photons were so entangled that the polarization of one is closely related to the orbital angular momentum of the other, which determines whether the wave photon travels to the left or to the right. Using these values as a proxy for the number of players, Aria and Brian won 93.84% of the 1,075,930 rounds, exceeding the maximum hidden variable of 88.89%. While not perfect, our 93.84% win rate is above what classical statistics would allow, demonstrating that physical reality is not fixed and can be manipulated by quantum entanglement. Quantum entanglement with "pseudo-telepathy." Indigestible "reality"? Or is it better to talk about almost unbelievable simulations?

We have discovered the oldest galaxy ever seen in the universe. A team of astronomers analyzed this image of the galaxy as if it were 13.5 billion years old. It is therefore the closest object to the Big Bang ever seen. This new discovery was announced by an international team of astronomers who analyzed recent observational data and sent their results to our agency. Dubbed Crystal, the galaxy dates to 300 million years after the Big Bang, about 100 million years earlier than any galaxy seen so far. Older galaxies tend to be the most distant because the universe has not stopped expanding since its birth. We are probably seeing the most distant starlight we have ever seen. Crystal existed at the earliest epoch of the universe. However, its exact age is unknown, as it may have formed in the first 300 million years. Crystal was discovered in orbit in the first launch data from the observatory's main infrared imager. Moving through the spectrum of light, from the infrared to the visible spectrum, and beyond, galaxies appear as infinitesimal dots that are part of a larger picture of the cosmos, the so called "deep field." "The astronomical record is already collapsing and becoming more volatile. Yes, we tend to applaud only when science leads to clear peer review. Nevertheless, this looks very promising. Sydney Another team of astrophysicists led by the same team, working with the same data, has come to similar conclusions so far.

What's hiding in the infrared? One of the big hopes is the ability to find the first galaxies that formed after the Big Bang, 13.8 billion years ago. They are so far from Earth that when light reaches us, it is stretched by the expansion of the universe and shifts into the infrared portion of the light spectrum.

Sidney and his colleagues reviewed this infrared data from the distant universe, looking for distinctive features of very distant galaxies. Below a certain wavelength of the infrared threshold, all photons, or particles of light, are absorbed by the neutral cosmic hydrogen between the object and the observer. By using data collected through different infrared filters aimed at the same region of space, we can see where these photon dips occur and use them to determine what speculated about the existence of more distant galaxies. One is Crystal and the other is the not-so-old Vidrium. We looked for all the early data on this amazingly prominent galaxy, and these were by far the two systems with the most compelling features. Although the evidence is solid, there is still a lot of "work to be done" to confirm the findings. A detailed property point will measure that exact distance. For now, the distance assumption is based on what you can't see. It would be great if there was an answer to what we are seeing. Still, the team has already discovered surprising things about this early galaxy. One is its mass, the equivalent of a billion Sun-like stars, and given that it formed shortly after the Big Bang, it's "potentially very surprising, because we don't really know what to make of it."

It is very difficult to make superconductors at room temperature. DNA is conceived as the solution. A superconductor is a material that has no electrical resistance. The flow of electrons is unimpeded, which means that electricity can be transmitted without loss or release of heat. Making superconductors that work at room temperature would require major technological breakthroughs. However, our group of scientists now believes they have a solution. Not too cold, not too hot. Superconductivity has been known for a long time. Nevertheless, superconducting materials were first made at cryogenic temperatures. For example, Mercury needed to be four degrees above absolute zero to become superconducting.

Later, the discovery of cuprates and superconductivity at high temperatures was a great breakthrough. However, it wasn't ideal either. Little's superconductors toyed with the idea. However, failed to solve the problem. Our team now believes that this theoretical network of semiconducting carbon nanotubes can be modified to drive chemical reactions along these nanotubes. What's the secret? DNA. Megan is working in cryo-electron microscopy, and the answer to this question lies in DNA. Using this material, they were able to use this advanced chemistry to create precise structures as tiny constructs at the molecular level. The result is a network of carbon nanotubes properly assembled to obtain the dream superconductor at room temperature. Test, test, and test. The network they created using DNA has not yet been tested in the field of superconductivity. Nevertheless, we believe it is evidence that this avenue has great future potential. So far, cryo-EM has become a dominant technique for determining the atomic structure of protein assemblies in biology. However, so far it has not impacted materials science. A revolution is coming. The impact of the discovery of room-temperature superconductors will be enormous in all fields. Power plants could be built far from cities; fusion reactors could be built closer; computers and electric motors could also find applications. and magnetic levitation devices such as spacecraft. The applications are exceptional and this breakthrough could help achieve them.

Now, folks, follow me as I show you a groundbreaking marvel. What is this doctor? This is the first computer made from human brain cells, much better than AI.

Artificial intelligence is almost the holy grail of future technology. There is no big company or university that is not working on developing artificial intelligence. Superior performance of the biological brain is often a role model. However, this is also a lot of work.

Our research involves the development of a sensor that interacts with brain cells using electrical signals. They were used to create quantum computers. A neural interface? It's quite similar. What are the basics of its manufacture? This is a breakthrough in biotechnology and nanotechnology. However, this is still a work in progress. The human brain is made up of billions of cells that communicate via chemical and electrical signals. Wireless nanosensors can be directly connected to the brain, allowing the dynamics of these brain signals to be monitored and manipulated. These nanosensors are flexible and microfabricated in dense arrays, allowing large amounts of information to be collected in the body for long periods of time. Our scientific team details how these devices are microengineered and their practical applications, such as enhancing organ functioning.

In this way, our development team hopes to save hours of tedious manufacturing and building and embed brain cells into computers. It may sound silly. However, their The first prototypes are already learning faster than traditional computer artificial intelligence.

How did you do that? That is exactly what we are going to talk about today. This biological intelligence precisely solves problems that artificial intelligence cannot. This is the use of genetically modified organisms by artificial intelligence That is correct. Have you developed MBI? Yes, I understand. For over

800 million years, evolution has trained the biological brains of humans and animals to act in real time, perceive unknown situations, and make the right decisions to survive. Each brain cell communicates with other neurons through thousands of connections, each capable of creating new neurons, breaking them down, or weakening them. It adapts and learns from experience at the same time, without the need for any hardware or large databases. All of these functions are already included in neuron biology.

The resulting nervous system is highly complex yet robust, powerful, and efficient. These are exactly the properties that computer scientists have long wanted to reproduce. So I created an artificial neural network made up of many small computers interconnected. They are designed to mimic brain function. It took decades to develop a processor and memory with the ability to enhance artificial intelligence because it was initially so difficult. You don't have to wait that long. We already have the first prototype. Meet Beth! Beth? Yes, a transhuman biological entity. Hidden MBI! Mixed biointelligence! As we know it now, deep neural networks are rapidly changing our world, whether artificial intelligence or other scientists prefer it. You are no match for Beth. It's still not a candidate for our brains! You're wrong!

Mixed biointelligence and computer scientists continue to work on developments such as human and animal reinforcement learning methods that allow AI to learn to make decisions. For example, she can learn how to play games on the hardware she's working on just by playing them on her site. Called neuromorphic computing, it aims to use small spikes of voltage to communicate information, much like neurons do, making artificial neural networks faster and more efficient than traditional GPU graphics processing units. I hope.

Furthermore, significant efforts are made to imitate the organic mind, which also lags behind as a minimum in most instances; however, wait a minute, why not simply pass all of the improvement work and join an organic community right into a laptop you noticed that appears to be crazy science? To begin with, a few questions arise: are brains and computers even compatible on the one hand? You have a logical laptop device product of software program hardware and memory storage imposing transistor era. A laptop is essentially made to resolve mathematics operations. On the other hand, you've got an organically grown community of neurons in which no borders among hardware, software, and garage are existent. Apprehensive structures have advanced to make complicated selections and produce them to move speedily at the same time as a laptop has no trouble calculating large numbers. Most people have difficulty simply multiplying four digit numbers in trade; we can walk and speak at the same time without the need to connect ourselves to large, significant, extraordinary computer systems; however, despite the large opposites, the link between mind and device can work. The key phrase is "mind device interfaces." In a nutshell, it's simply brief voltage spikes. We can already measure and cause those movement potentials by attaching electrodes to the mind and using brief voltages from outside. Each enter and output can be performed via the identical electrodes. Now we simply need to connect a laptop in to research and manipulate the neural interest nicely.

The mind device interface is prepared for movement. Despite the fact that mind-device interfaces have been researched for a long time, only the cochlear implant has made it to mass adoption. There are also experimental tasks in which members can manipulate prostheses simply with their minds. For instance, neural connections are currently running on a mind-device interface, which, of course, might be capable of doing the whole lot sooner or later. This monkey, for instance, can play thoughts pong with it. So those are a few proofs that the hyperlink between mind and device is possible. However, the scientists at cortical labs want to integrate a remote organic community into a computer. That's far from kumbaya! Now, no longer the complete mind, that could be a piece of it and a standard to position it. Evidently, they need to combine mind cells right into a motherboard like a photo card. To accomplish that, first off, they need to place it in a small, controllable environment. Secondly, they need to make certain to alter the one mind cell into the interface of a laptop. Multi-electrode arrays come into play. Those are circuit forums with dozens of touch factors on those forums. As an example, you could flatten arrangements like slices of mind cells. At some stage in this test, the touchy tissue is saved at the proper temperature and implemented with a nutrient answer that.

Additionally, it incorporates oxygen to nourish the brain cells with this method. Neuroscientists have located lots that approximately the capability of neurons. The arrangements defined herein nevertheless come from animals which, alas, need to die for those experiments. However, current technological know-how already has an answer to this moral hassle. It's referred to as pluripotent stem cells. They can take those from animal embryos or higher from human pores and skin so that no animals are involved in the trials any longer. With the proper processing, they are able to make neurons out of those stem cells, which may be brought to the multi-electrode array and, with the proper electric stimulation, they are able to subsequently manipulate the boom of those enterprises. Cortical labs integrated organic brain cells into a computer. They named their invention "Dish Mind." No, they do not serve you brains in a dish. It is the simplest ironic method of all the scientists. The query now could be how cortical labs checked and approved this gadget. As you already found out, the usual way to check those mastering structures is the outstanding high-give up sport referred to as pong. With a purpose to play pong, our mini cyborg mind wishes something like a show as an output and the opportunity to go into inputs, essentially something like a controller. In this example, the Australian group described a square place on the board as a show with the distinction that no pixels light up. However, the neurons get electric stimulation through electrodes and the enter operates. In addition, the scientists have described a place in which the neural interest is measured and decided. If the neural interest of the neurons had been better on one aspect, the paddle of the pong game shifted up. If the focus had been on the other side, the paddle would have shifted down and as a poor remark. They simply inspired all of the neurons at the same time. When they ignored a ball, it became the first time in records that this was ever investigated, and the mini cyborg even did a truly appropriate activity. The community of organic mind cells began to research pong in only a few minutes. The machine with mind cells of a mouse first did worse than the machine with mind cells of a mouse. However, then discovered quicker and did higher on the stop improbable how each organic structure discovered pong with fewer repetitions than the ai of classical computer systems. Certainly, the ai changed into nevertheless higher at gambling pong in the long run. Nevertheless, to be honest, we ought to remember that the mind computer includes just a few hundred neurons, even as the human mind, then again, owns 86 billion, so there may be a large capability for scaling this machine and the very last phrases concerning overall performance have now no longer been spoken.

The team has just concluded this study and defined those mind cells to be included in the review. Therefore the community has essentially an idea that it's miles to the pedal. However, surely some hundred cells truly have no cognizance and no idea of themselves or their function in a digital world in any respect. Thus far, the test has only been posted as a preprint, which means we do not know whether or not the test has already been reviewed by impartial professionals and will be posted in a legit science journal in its contemporary way. However, a few professionals have already spoken to a few newshounds. The improvement of organic neural networks is surely in its inception. The large amount of time required to supply and perform the structures is a significant challenge for this generation. In the long run, the stem cells ought to be cultivated and stored alive on the circuit board so that you may not be placing gadgets of organic mind cells into your pocket and being attentive to your playlist every time. However, it is possible that someday these structures will be combined into massive computing servers that we will be able to access remotely, or they may find use in self-sufficient robots like cyborgs, androids, and others. We can wait and see what fate has in store for us. However, one crucial question remains unanswered: how does a community even solve a concrete problem in the first place? A mind or a deep neural community is sort of a black box; you understand what comes in and what comes out. However, you don't know on which logical foundation the problem is solved. Nobody can pick out the decision-making in this sort of field without evidence or correct it before it makes a critiquing. Some of you may be wondering if using these mini-brains for research purposes is ethical. Imagine developing consciousness and being trapped in a computer playing ping-pong. Probably not, Although ethically important questions remain, as after a certain number of neurons, these systems can naturally develop consciousness and emotion. What do you think of this technology? Do we need to explore more for humanity? Or do you think this is a bit too far?

The new artificial neurons are a million times faster than the human brain. Our multidisciplinary team of researchers set out to push the speed limits of artificial analog synapses, a key component of "analog deep learning." They have successfully created analog synapses that are millions of times faster than the human brain, according to the agency's press release. As scientists venture to the cutting edge of machine learning, the time, energy, and money needed to train increasingly complex neural network models skyrockets.

Deep learning is a new branch of artificial intelligence that promises faster computations and consumes less energy. It comes in deep learning applications. Analog processors need programmable registers just as digital processors need transistors. According to the press release, these resistors, when properly configured, can be used to create synapse networks and analog neurons. The newly developed materials are now compatible with silicon fabrication techniques and can pave the way for integration into commercial computing hardware for deep learning applications. This important discovery has made possible the powerful nanofabrication technology that enables us to combine these components and demonstrate that these devices are inherently very fast and operate at reasonable voltages.

"This work makes these devices look very promising for future applications," he added. Human brain synapses fire more quickly than animal brain synapses. By abandoning the commonly used organic medium in favor of a high-tech glass known as inorganic phosphosilicate glass (PSG), the researchers were able to achieve nanosecond speeds. Scientists say that it is about one million times faster than synapses in the human brain. In a statement, scientist Professor Stephen said, "A voltage difference of about 0.1 volts is limited by the stability of water, so action potentials in living cells rise and fall on a time scale of milliseconds."

Here we apply up to 10 volts to a special nanometer-thick glass film that conducts protons without causing permanent damage. And the stronger the electric field, the faster the ionic device. They are faster than analog and digital counterparts. Analog deep learning is faster and more energy efficient than digital deep learning, primarily for two reasons. As the statement explains, "First, computations are performed in memory, so large amounts of data never pass back and forth between memory and the processor." Moreover, analog processors can also perform parallel processing. As the die size increases, the analog processor no longer needs time to complete new operations because all calculations are performed simultaneously. A key component of new analog processor technology is known as programmable proton resistors. These resistors are measured in nanometers and arranged in a board-like array inspired by the human brain.

It's common knowledge that learning occur in the human brain by strengthening and weakening connections, the synapses between neurons. Deep neural networks have long followed this approach. In this approach, network weights are programmed using a training algorithm. This new processor enables analog machine learning by increasing and decreasing the electrical conductivity of the proton resistors. promising results. The result of these new analog synapses are programmable recordings that significantly speed up neural network training while significantly reducing the cost and energy required to perform this process. "Once you have an analog processor, you stop training networks that other people are working on." In other words, it's about spaceships, not faster cars. Applications for the new devices range from autonomous cars to fraud detection and medical image analysis.

IV. The secret code

A car in the middle of a busy highway is found by a traffic patrol. An odd scene that no one has the faintest idea of what may have occurred. The driver is nowhere around. The vehicle is still on and, what is baffling, it indicates a speed of 130 mph! How is that possible if it is not moving? Its battery is almost dead. Yes, it is an electric vehicle. It was reported a couple of hours ago by a traffic police officer passing by. Feds came to the site to take the car using a tow truck that would take it away for further investigation. Police officers are checking the plates to identify the owner.
Sydney appeared a touch downhearted at the end of the week. The young scientist at least seemed buoyed by the painstaking pace of her work. She is decoding an old manuscript. What's this? I have some missed calls from the wee hours. I didn't notice this before. Naim called me! This is really weird. We are not that close. It doesn't make sense at all. It should have been an emergency. I must find out about it. I will call him. After several attempts, he doesn't pick it up. It seems it was turned off. This is getting more intriguing. I will ask his assistant about his whereabouts.
Hey, doc! What's up, Emmett? Everything's fine. I just dropped by to see how the translation is going. Not very well. Things got really slow after they picked up fast at the very beginning of the month. I know, that's how these things turn out to be. Who sent you over here, Emmett? You are very straightforward, Sydney. You can bet on that. The agency is concerned about the codex. Don't go beating around the bush. Spit your guts out. They wanted me to come and make sure that you are on the right track. What does that

mean? It means that if you are not making any progress, I should bring some other scientists in. What for? They would take over your job. Listen, that won't happen. I am close to a great breakthrough. How close are you? I know what you came here for. What was that? Just to pressure me and push my work forward. You know what, that doesn't have any effect on me. Just turn around and tell them to go somewhere else to bother other people. You know that I cannot do that. It's true. Sorry, I was carried by the emotions. Emmett leaves her alone to allow for things to settle down. He will return later on to catch upon her.

Parallel universes and the spirit world world, along with the afterlife are intertwined dimensions invisible to the naked eye. Science has made rapid progress in recent years decoding the human genome and space exploration has brought new insights toward other universes, worlds, dimensions, including the quantum-verse. Stephen didn't knock at her door and unexpectedly asked, "Does that comprise the world inside us?" Yes, it does. Oh, I didn't hear you were around here. Surely I am. What was all that? The human body possesses a secret code. While the existence of parallel universes seems completely inconsistent with modern science, recent research suggests that these worlds may actually exist. As a great proponent of quantum mechanics, I am particularly interested in this topic. What does all this have to do with our genome and the universe? Everything, even the spiritual or sacred realm, is connected to us through a sacred code. Show me!

Sydney reads, "God's DNA is in every heir of God's kingdom." That's quite a revelation! DNA is the molecule that contains all the information necessary for the effective development of each person. This is the divinity of all humans. And we have inherited a sacred code for us. What does that imply? It may indicate that atoms, DNA, and data coding work together to give us a code of codes. Thus, our task is to decode the information at the atomic and molecular level of our DNA. It is essential to access the sacred code. How is information encoded in binary systems and stored in our DNA molecules? Deoxyribonucleic acid, or DNA, is the molecule responsible for storing and transmitting genetic information in living organisms. DNA itself is a storehouse of biological data. It was only a matter of time before the secret code stored in our DNA was deciphered. This is not necessarily biological. DNA molecules are made up of small units called nucleotides. Each nucleotide then consists of a simple sugar (pentose), a nitrogenous base, and a phosphate remainder. Each nucleotide unit can have four different nitrogenous bases: A, T, G, or C. There we go again. What? The lecture on genetics is an endless flow of information that is usually futile. Come one, don't be so tough on me! It is at least trivial to me. All right, I will summarize it.

For convenience, the entire nucleotide unit can be named with the same letter that identifies the nitrogenous base it contains. Therefore, a DNA molecule is composed of only four types of nucleotides: A, T, G, and C. Basically, the DNA molecule has the form of a code that uses the four-letter binary codes A, T, G, and C, composed of 0 and 1. (0,1) DNA, in this case, is a unit of information and, unlike bits, which use two numbers 0 and 1, DNA uses four letters: A, T, G, and C. Each bit can have two possible values (0 or 1) and each nucleotide can have four possible values (A, T, G, and C), so theoretically each nucleotide has two bits, i.e., per nucleotide. Up to 2 bits can be encoded. However, nucleotides have no real capacity to store two bits. This is because DNA molecules contain long sequences of repeated nucleotides, such as: baaaaaaaaaaa... Alternatively, a high GC nucleotide content is not practical as it is not synthetically stable and leads to coding errors. Therefore, we estimate the actual storage capacity of a nucleotide to be about 1.83 bits. Are you trying to store data in DNA? It's been done for a long time now. What's trending is getting the largest capacity of storage. I see!

And at that point, you may wonder how this genius works. All this is possible thanks to a brilliant combination of biology and mathematics. Any kind of information can be encoded in a binary system of 0's and 1's. In this case, operating systems, movies, computer viruses, and e-books are first encrypted in a binary system. The next step is to convert the information obtained in binary code into the DNA nucleotide code: A, T, G, and C. Nucleotides or those containing many GC nucleotides are not allowed.

Scientists have successfully applied mathematical algorithms to solve these problems. These are a series of mathematical transformations that make it possible to encode the zeros and ones of the letters A, T, G, and C, using repetitive combinations of consecutive letters and avoiding using a large number of letters. GC. Having encoded everything in the sequence, does this suggest that humans added the name of God to the DNA? Chances are, my friend. And what significance does this name have in our DNA? We tend to see what we want when it comes to religious beliefs. Are we talking about "Pareidolia?" Yes, indeed. A cloud may look like an angel. With very little effort, you will find that a certain order of numbers can produce the name you want in the language of your choice. Especially when it comes to an ancient language, such a theory gives you some validity. Oh, Stephen, how cynically sensitive you are today! Boastfully yours, darling! There is no reason not to. What's more, did Sydney delay the purely theoretical question of where we should provide the secret code for use? It could not be determined. Intervention from another world is required. Something divine? Let's say at least from a hyper-advanced extraterrestrial civilization telling us what to do with these numbers and name. You're correct again.

Besides, the letters A, T, G, and C are used to synthesize the DNA molecule formed by this sequence of nucleotides. Thus, we have a physical medium, a DNA molecule, as a disk or disc. This synthesized DNA contains information about operating systems, movies, and computer viruses and can be transported as a flash drive, CD, external hard disk, or other form of data storage. All of those are obsolete nowadays. That's true. To obtain the information from the DNA molecule, as well as the binary code of 0 and 1, a reverse data decoding process is applied, translating the letter codes A, T, G, and C into operating systems, movies, and computer viruses. Is this breakthrough impressive? I don't think so. This smells like a scam out of nowhere. One of the criteria for this study is that we were able to store 60% more data than any previous research. In addition, we were able to make the encoding and decoding processes run error-free.

However, it should be noted that when they get excited about these studies, they tend to exaggerate to get funding to continue their studies. Are scientists so contradictory? Our community has it all. It will be a few more years before this technology reaches our homes, or DNA "hard drives." At the moment, this cryptanalytic system is very expensive and takes too long to retrieve the information.

One characteristic of DNA is that it contains the codes necessary for the development and functioning of all living things. Nowadays, however, it is very common to hear or read about the concept "it's in our DNA" outside of a medical or biological context. Sportsmen, politicians, businessmen, etc., use it when they want to highlight your qualities or behavior. They fall into the error of using DNA as a carrier of all information, carrying only what uniquely identifies us, while underestimating such an important environmental issue as education. It provides a wealth of information and guidance.

In addition to biological data, the encoding of digital data in DNA is also a developing topic, highlighting the advantages of this molecule as a storage medium over current physical media. Thus, the ability of DNA molecules to form ultra-compact structures is well known, allowing them to store large amounts of information in a very small space. Does this code contain ancient information and instructions on how to live our lives? You've come a long way. Come on, I don't think it's a manual for life.

On the other hand, under optimal conditions of temperature and humidity, DNA offers a long shelf life, potentially hundreds of thousands of years, much longer than today's means of storing data. Finally, in addition to its evolutionary guarantee of non-loss, it is not expected to be an obsolete carrier, so we know better every day how to increase the efficiency of DNA synthesis and reading. It can scale up in a few years. Given the needs created by this kind of information avalanche, all this lays the groundwork for treating DNA as an alternative form of digital data storage. However, the results obtained until recently have not been entirely satisfactory, and the development of methods to achieve this is still in its infancy.

Despite these attractive results, the systematic use of this methodology is still in its infancy, as important technical limitations remain to be solved. Perhaps most importantly is the cost of this process, because although DNA synthesis and readout have become exponentially cheaper in recent years, it still presents a real obstacle. Synthesized for six converted DNA files, each 200 bases in length. The files were restored without error as described. This signifies a complete success. This encoding strategy then achieved 215 petabytes of data in 1 gram of DNA. This is 100 times faster than other methods. DNA is the new computing architecture.

After all her efforts and attempts to decode the message underneath our DNA, Sydney has discovered a hidden language in the human genetic code. It is in our DNA , which tells the cell how to regulate genes. Until now, this language was hidden beneath the code that controls protein synthesis. However, because both codes work together, the findings may lead to new interpretations of genetic information and its relationship to health and disease.

This code contains information that could change our interpretation of genetic instructions, allowing us to better interpret mutations to better understand health and disease. This is a comprehensive human genome project aimed at finding where and how patterns for biological function are conserved in our genes. The findings will be presented in detail in the minutes of the last meeting of the institution.

Furthermore, a second hidden language was deciphered, and it was hypothesized that it governs only one organic process, protein synthesis. This synthesis follows the patterns set by the sequence of nucleotides, the organic molecules present in the messenger RNA mRNA that contain the genetic information of DNA. Surprisingly, he also discovered that the genome uses the genetic code for other purposes. It is actually "writing" in two languages. One of those languages, as they say, describes how proteins are formed. The other tells cells how to control genes. It is also suspected that there is a third language used to store data in the system. However, what data is important enough to store in your own body? The largest knowledge base in existence A secret code or whatever you want to call it. This is amazing!

In addition, Sidney claims that one of these "languages" is written on top of the other, which explains why the latter remained hidden for so long. There must be a third thin layer underneath both. For years, we have assumed that changes in DNA that affect the genetic code only affect protein composition. We know that this basic assumption about the interpretation of the human genome is biased. The new results show that DNA is an incredibly powerful information storage device and that nature has reached its full potential in unexpected ways. Protein-coding genes are generally composed of units called "codons," and each codon consists of a triplet of nucleotides. Codons are the basic units of information in protein synthesis processes.

After discovering "three different languages" in the genetic code, we were astonished: 15% of the genetic material from which proteins are derived has this second function. They therefore act as anchor sites for drugs that regulate gene activity. So we can use the same genetic code not only to produce proteins but also to determine how many to produce. This work is interesting and provocative. We are talking about a new dimensional map of the human genome. The finger that turns the genes of neurons on and off is the hand of God. There are many genetic variants associated with an increased risk of developing diseases that do not alter proteins, misleading the scientific community, i.e., producing 100%, 50%, or 0% of the total protein. If a mutation was found that did not involve a change in the protein sequence, it was ignored. Revisit the analyses of the genomes of lethal diseases, as this mutation may affect a second code and, therefore, the regulation of another gene associated with these developments is necessary. From an evolutionary perspective, this military layer of information should have helped protect the nucleotides, the chemical letters that make up DNA, against the constant assault of natural selection. This would have made them an integral part of evolution.

A human secret code with a third layer that hides the real information of the creator; the whole algorithm of creation is created or simulated, evolutionary or degenerate. Because one code is written on top of another, the second is hidden for a long time, and the third can only be discovered by deciphering letters into numbers and deciphering these into binary messages. The second code produces the sacred code.

Genetic engineering has made it easy for scientists to make huge progress in decoding the human genome, and they have now found evidence of God in our DNA code. However, what is it that the code found in the DNA code leads us to believe in the existence of a divinity? DNA is located in the nucleus of every cell. It instructs the computer clock to perform all the functions that take place within the cells of the body, just like cells are in our bodies, via incredibly complex and very long codes. Nevertheless, how did this complex DNA code convince scientists of the existence of a creator? We're still trying to understand it.

Hidden within our DNA is another code that contains information that changes the way scientists read the instructions contained in our DNA and how we see the universe. Since the genetic code was deciphered, scientists believe that its sole purpose is to write information about proteins, not external information about science, life, and the universe. We were all surprised to discover that the genome uses genetic codes to describe three different languages. The new results show that DNA is "an information storage device that is a kind of super hard drive in the universe, something incredibly powerful that nature has unleashed to its full potential in unexpected ways," it is emphasized. The genetic code uses a 64-letter alphabet called "codons."

Megan is running to the parking lot. Something happened to Naim. All his colleagues are not aware of that, something unusual occurred during the dawn hours to him. He must have been obliged to get off his car and who know what happened afterwards.

Sydney tells Steph, "I know I need to optimize my time by focusing myself on the biggest task at hand, without any distractions, like this one." What do you have so far? After a blistering attempt, you won't believe it. Just try me! God's name is encoded in our DNA. Seriously? Yes. How come? I cannot tell you how, not yet. Where is it? What does that mean to our research? It is on the sulfuric bridge in the sequence of 10-5-6-5. Do you need any extra help? No, I don't. I can get you some experts on ancient languages. No, way! What about some genetic engineers? No, no, no! I will continue alone. Okay, take it easy. Whatever you say, Sydney. Let's continue. This is an incredible discovery. Yes, it is. However, we're further off the pace than we hoped to comply with the time constraints to finish the decoding process as fast as the agency demands.

I have to get rid of all these thoughts and find peace of mind. The sacred code of our DNA, also known as the code of all codes, consists of the so-called hidden code of our genome. What do you get from this code? Perhaps the knowledge of the whole universe? In all the sacred books, they tell stories of past, present, and future events, and this code is hidden implicitly... not at first glance. Sidney was able to access the most relevant parts of the entire universe thanks to encryption rules that could only be applied to ancient Hebrew texts using advanced computer programs with artificial intelligence. Some of the most famous scientists and decryption experts have conducted their own tests to reveal the truth behind the messages hidden in our DNA. The way we extract meaningful messages is by the order of letters and numbers in DNA. When a starting point and a distance are selected, a number will be displayed, which can be negative. From this starting point, the letters in the sequence are selected and translated. For example, the first time you decode it, you will see the following sentence:

The bold letters, read from left to right in four-letter intervals, form the word "Sacred Code." Ignore spaces and punctuation. A series of letters often contains several sequences on the same subject at the same time. This is because the text is arranged in a regular matrix with the same number of characters on each line, then rectangles are drawn. A "CODE" sequence is displayed. Usually, you only need to display one smaller rectangle. Characters are missing in this case. However, it is important that the number of missing characters is the same for each pair of adjacent lines. Otherwise, the sequence will not be executed. If you line up the letters of the human genome sequence, the words "sacred" and "encrypted" will appear. There are thousands of possible combinations, and they all produce the same result. Just get the code number and information on how to use it. Translations into other languages will follow later. Does this require belief in creationism? The influence of an omniscient being? Or perhaps just thank the whole universe for how carefully the sequence in our DNA was constructed. That is as complex as those in our bodies. It is no accident that our own bodies provide us with all the data instead. Admit that you don't. Anyone who says so knows nothing about deciphering.

The main objection to secret codes is that similar patterns are found in ancient books and sacred texts.

The odds of finding a string corresponding to a meaningful word in random locations are low. Nevertheless, there are so many possible distances from the starting point that even if evenly spaced words are separated by only two or a few letters, such words are expected. Finding them and relating them to each other is almost impossible. Proponents of the code argue that the sequences found in our DNA are superior and incomparable to those found in books. They are also investigating new types of code to address the criticisms. However, without an objective measure of quality and an objective method for selecting each piece of evidence, it is not possible to determine whether a particular observation is significant. Therefore, most skeptics' efforts are focused on refuting scientific claims. Sydney reveals this entire web of codes. She has traced the statistical discovery that a secret code for visual reading is written in the spiral. The results could not be explained on the grounds that the data was not selected correctly because it was extracted from a natural DNA sequence. The data was not clear because of the way the decoding was done.

Each word leads to the next word and number, which unlocks another layer of biological encryption. I cannot explain how many numbers related to data appear together.

The code hypothesis is tested. It is a reality now. When I try to reproduce the experiment, I get the same result. One technical problem that complicated our research was the enormous amount of information processed. We used a quantum computer, and it worked perfectly. After understanding the dynamics of the code, we have accomplished in days what would have taken a conventional computer millions of years.

After this stage, there is going to be an ongoing discussion to see how we got the code. And we know the preliminary results are promising. The rest of the team doesn't have all the information. The government is withholding it.

There are some prophetic messages embedded in our DNA, they are still to be fulfilled. This hidden code predicts a nuclear holocaust or some sort of global catastrophe that had not yet occurred. Keep on decoding, don't stop now! I'm exhausted, though.

We are all in a constant whirlwind of emotions, experiences, situations, conflicts, and still learning. Despite decoding the divine code is a long made decision to take us to a higher level of civilization, it is shocking how we incarnate the container, and the code has lived in us for so long. We have just been the vessel. Since our bodies, planets, galaxies, and universes are made of the same cosmic dust, the same material and we are inseparable, there are some assumptions that seem to be the right deduction. Thus, what's valid for us may be so for the rest. Don't jump at any conclusions yet.

We are energy, vibration, and frequency, we can reprogram ourselves and get out of the system. We exist in three realms or dimensions; the physical world, the mental reality, and the spiritual realm. Our consciousness goes beyond those planes.

In recent years, I have had the impression that time passes faster than before. The hustle and bustle of everyday life starts as soon as you wake up in the morning and ends the next morning when you start all over again. This vortex takes us away from ourselves and makes us forget that time is actually the monotonous programming that separates us. Therefore, when we discover simulation, it is a sacred moment when our beloved divinity can manifest in infinite ways and we understand its message. Our time is mundane and dizzying, shaped by the hands of the clock and daily tasks.

When we are in trouble, we go to the center and call upon our voice, our inner voice, and ask for intervention using techniques we have learned through meditation, prayer, breathing, and visualization. In one way or another, we all pause, take a breath, in our routines to first ask for your help, then thank you, and finally wait. It is in this last instance that instead of waiting calmly, we let fear and despair flow, arise within us, taking us even further away from what we were looking for. It brings us into absolute harmony and gives us the perfect moment to incarnate in the physical world. It is time to reveal the the next part of the sequence, I have a hunch that it will finally unveil the code of codes to us.

Four nuclide acids bind the DNA helices together by sulfuric bridges in the sequence of A-T-C-G-EVERY 10, 5, 6, 5 acids 10 5   6   5   10 Hebraic numeric meaning. 10 5 6 5 Y-H-V-H (יהוה) The Bridge, bond, glue that holds the human DNA sequence together. Are you still with me, Steph? You sort of got me lost. Where? Somewhere in between the sequence. How can you get letters and numbers? Isn't it spectacular? No, not if I don't understand it. That's a long story, my friend. I don't have the time to explain it to you. I just follow my gut. I should do the same. Are we talking about the same thing? Never mind.

Nothing is lost in the universe by casualty. Why did you say that, Sydney? Steph, come closer. She approached him and kissed him wildly. Why? Haven't you realized this? What? My feelings for you. To be honest, I also like you a lot. However, work keeps me apart from my family and from anything that is fun. That shouldn't be. They both took the afternoon off and went to a sordid motel to spend time together. There is too much strict work and orders, aliens, codes, and everything else. Their phones were silenced. They kept on drinking until the day light closed in. It is time that we go back to boredom. I mean, to our reality. Sure. Gosh! How would we have figured this out? This is unbelievable!

Sydney got back to her laboratory. I've got a name! Yes, indeed. This same name is present in many ancient texts as "Yhbh." It has no vowels. This is flabbergasting. There's still more. What else? This is carved into our DNA, it reads: "This is why I personally don't use the name of the son or solely use the title of God." The word God is used in another part of the sequence as "Elohiym" with a few variations. What variations? That's what I had been working on before you interrupted my work. Don't blame it on me!

A couple of hours later, Emmett calls the agency and tells them, "She tries to bite off more than she can chew." What do you suggest? I recommend the agency send more seasoned scientists to help her speed up this research. It is a sensitive matter. Hence I encourage you to secure the perimeter and control any personnel accessing the laboratory. Understood.

Sydney didn't give a lot of thought to her unexpected visitor. Since it is my understanding that "YHVH" is the father's name, the Greek translation versus a transliteration of their names cannot be sustained in my honest opinion. "YOCHANON" I could be wrong in interpreting this verse. I should follow Emmett's advice and get some scholars who could help me interpret these verses. No, I shouldn't concede to the agency that. It would be an acknowledgment of my incompetence to complete this task. What if I tell Stephen? He has a really brilliant mind, and it's fine as long as I continue to learn from others. Nevertheless, it wouldn't make sense at all. These names are very similar." I'm in trouble. I really need help, maybe from outside this world. Uh, it is always the same assuage disappointment. The agency will bring a coveted scientist to take over my job. Hold your horses Sydney! No, I won't let them. I'm almost there. I have the numbers. I will input the rest of the information into the quantum computer. I am afraid of what may pop up on the screen. Oh my gosh! Here it is, the code!

Mr. Andrews looked away and closed the door. There is no outstanding ending as to what really happened to Dr. Naim. The federal government is revising all the surveillance cameras along the route Naim took that ill-fated morning. Look at this! He arrived at the gas station on the highway. Later, two guys got close to him! I took some pictures of the video, frame by frame. That's fabulous! Can you enlarge them? Okay, let me adjust the settings. The photo quality is very bad. These blurry images must be sent to our technicians for improvement. Sure, right away. As they continue to search for other videos, they come across footage of one of the men who was in Naim's car. This is the first evidence we obtained. Highway cameras did not capture the exact moment of the disappearance. However, there is a warehouse nearby. Get the video from their cameras as soon as possible. In the meantime, let's access traffic cameras further along the road. There should be something in these videos. After hours of scanning videos, they finally got a video of a stranger helping Naim out of his car. He dragged Naim into an SUV. Can you get the license plate number? No, I can't. I will follow it with other cameras along the road until I can zoom in on the plate. Well done! What about his automobile report? The guys at the laboratory just finished the analysis. What did they find? The radiation levels are skyrocketing! What do you mean? We couldn't measure it accurately. Isn't there a device that can measure radiation in a car? The radiation level exceeded their capacity. Why? It outperforms all detectors. How many have you tried? We've tried 3 so far. At first, I thought it was over 100 mSv. However, it was over 400–600 mSv. A final measurement showed it to be much more radioactive. We sent the floor mat residues to the laboratory to identify the material. What is that? It's a cosmic mineral that we don't know about. Please contact Mr. Andrews for permission to obtain more information from the space agency or to apply for a search warrant. That's not necessary.

A couple of months ago, Dr. Faith was contacted by some religious figure to arrange a meeting to have a mutually interesting conversation. She accepted the invitation and arrived at the appointment on time. As she entered the main gate, a somber gentleman wearing a cassock greeted her. You will be received by our bishop now. Thanks. Dr. Faith! Hi, your

excellency, Graziano! Please forget about the formalities. Sure. What can I do for you? You know that the church is the house of sinners. I thought that you were all saints. No, you are wrong. We are far from perfection. We receive everyone who has sinned. I'm pretty sure you didn't call me to come to your presence to give me a lecture on theology. That's correct. We have a problem that is growing by the minute and we think that you can solve it. Me? Yes, you and your crew. What is that? Many developed countries are becoming atheists and almost their whole populations are turning their back on religion and getting away from church. That's devastating. Sort of! Why? Every challenge provides us an opportunity to prove what we are made of. That's a valid point. However, I still don't get what I can do for you. Can you create an artificial genetic code? Um... Creating an artificial genetic code is viable. In fact, we have created it several times. With what purpose? It is for storing data and encrypting messages for Cybersecurity reasons. That sounds great to me! Tell me more about the options we have and I will let you know what our original idea is to exploit some loopholes, let's say in the cosmos. Okay, that's fair.
First, the method exists, and we can surely satisfy your wishes. It is not my wish, it is a divine will. Yes, of course. Whatever you say. What exactly do you want us to code in the DNA? What about God's name? That's not so complicated. What options do you offer us, Dr. Faith? The simplest cipher is created by using an encryption table or code to convert one character into another. Knowing the code makes the original message to be easily deciphered. Thus, it's common to change the code often to make decryption more

complicated. This is music for my ears. Since biologists discovered the code a few decades ago, that made possible to decipher the genetic information of living beings, and ultimately can enhance new techniques to modify the code itself. It's stunning what science can do for us today. Is there another way to accomplish our mission? Yes, there is some sort of experimental technique. However, it is worth the while. Please give me the details. Our research group previously developed an artificial translation system, named the "DIVINE" system. I approve of the name. They both laughed. However, this artificial translation system fail the very moment you attempt incorporating in vitro transcribed tRNAs instead of natural one. This is because of chemically modified bases. Because some of these modifications are not easy to replicate in vitro, the research team hypothesized that if they selected those tRNAs that could either function or show relatively little loss of function without the chemical modifications, they may be able to successfully reconstitute protein synthesis with their pure "divine" system using only in vitro transcribed tRNAs.

What else can you offer us? Perhaps something powerful will astound humanity. Scientists have demonstrated an incredible ability to manipulate the building blocks of life using advanced genetic techniques. By altering the order of atoms in DNA and rewriting the human genetic code, which is the same as saying that you have successfully altered the divine instructions for life as we know it.

The other is edited RNA, which is a chemical cousin of DNA and unlocks the information in the genetic code. It has been described as clever, important, and exciting. Altering the molecular structure is a key technique to convert one into another. Researchers can now manipulate the four bases. However, there are still issues around safety and implementation: Having a machine that can create the change you want to make is only the start. You still need to do all this other work. Nevertheless, having the machine really helps. Sure, it does. That's the beginning of a new partnership.

DNA is the master copy, the blueprint of our genetic code. However, in order for a cell to use the genetic instructions, it must first create an RNA copy. It is very similar to visiting a library without access to reading any of the books. You are only allowed to use digital versions of scanned books. The researchers used their RNA approach to correct an inherited form of anemia in human cells. That's a good cause.

All of the experiments were on human cells growing in the laboratory with mRNA and were promising. I strongly recommend we use this technique. How would it be effectively applied? What about a vaccine? Wouldn't it be obvious that most people wouldn't take it? Not if you first create the need for it. A fake need? Isn't it a fake proof of your religion? You are very clever, Dr. Faith. So are you. All right, then we have an agreement. Take care of the genetic manipulation. You mean the "vaccine." Yes, it is better if we call it like that. Sure. Then, I will take care of the rest. I agreed. You are dismissed, Dr. Faith. Please do not contact me. Off the record, I have never met you in my life. I don't think we will see each other again. That may be true. I will send some of my assistants to you. Moreover, you will be rewarded for your great deeds on behalf of our faith.

As Dr. Faith leaves the bishop's office, she has in mind who's going to work on the coding. Naim? He's brilliant and discreet. What's more, he doesn't have the exposure to the media that other scientists in our team do have. I can split the research and the application. Thus, Sydney may be the best fit for the research, and Naim will apply the code to the vaccine. None of them should know what they are doing separately. I will make sure that doesn't happen, because it could jeopardize the whole operation. I can have Emmett supervise the research part and advertise it as the greatest breakthrough ever; and I will do the monitoring of the application myself to keep it secretly tight.

V. Consciousness and Fractals

Naim's peers at the laboratory were informed of the unusual event in which he disappeared. Moreover, they requested their discretion since the matter has been kept secret for now. Megan asked the detective Johnson, "What happened to Dr. Naim?" We don't really know, ma'am! We found his car and that's it! We are investigating the scene and all the people who were in touch with him. I hope he's still alive. Do you know what his most recent work was about? Of course, he works with me. We've been working on scientific projects that are classified. I cannot reveal anything about them. Then we'll get the search warrant to find out about it. Do what you have to do, sir. When Megan returned to the facilities, she knew that Naim must be alive and that he may have been kidnapped by some foreign government or terrorist organization. Whatever comes to my mind is just speculative. I will ask the top leaders of the agency what they know about it.

It was early Monday morning when the public learned, through a written statement from the federal agency, that scientist Naim Singha had been kidnapped. Hours later, agents executed a search warrant at his home and laboratory. Federal law enforcement would be better off looking for something very important. It seems that nuclear secrecy is at stake. Who did he talk to about this? It hasn't been revealed yet. Security breaches will undoubtedly backfire on space agency controls. Top-class highly classified documents related to nuclear weapons development, and top-sensitive compartmented information. These materials were among the items retrieved by agents in their searches of Naim's archives. This gives us a great incentive to retrieve this material as soon as possible. A freak hijacker may have tried to stop the car in the middle of a busy street while keeping the engine revving at a high speed under the disguise of an abduction. At the very least, we have to admit that the perpetrators had some imagination to set up the situation. In so doing, Mr. Andrews seeks to underscore government officials' deep concern over the type of information Naim believed may have been in his possession and may have fallen into the wrong hands.

Was Naim really kidnapped? We don't know that. According to our sources, he was involved in leaking classified documents. Which ones? I infer those are sensitive nuclear weapons documents, which he was working on regarding nuclear energy sources other than minerals of terrestrial origin. Wait a second! What exactly do you mean? He was experimenting with some alien sources! Non-mineral and alien elements can generate such power for any energy and weapon. Who would be interested in this information? Basically, foreign governments. Yes, that sounds plausible. However, who can pay for such information? Who are you talking about paying? Oh, you are right. Those who followed him only caught him by force. No, not at all. There is a high degree of intelligence behind this operation. It's done well, and there are no indications as to who stole what. What about his car? It's still a mystery! Was it a trick to fool us? Maybe. If so, they are really smart people in charge of running this operation. We do not take such threats lightly. The laboratory looked at some key issues that may have arisen from recent developments. How serious must these actions have been? Has national security been compromised? If told to come up with the worst-case scenario possible, it would be very dangerous for him to improperly and illegally take it home or share it with foreign agents in exchange for money or scientific secrets. It's just a guess at this point.

Do you believe aliens were involved in Naim's disappearance? No, I don't think so. You wouldn't have left such a mess. This vehicle was left there on purpose to get their message across. Which message? They escaped murder. No wild garlic was sought, so we dismiss the kidnapping theory. Due to the nature of the operation, no saucers were seen near the crime scene, so no aliens were involved. What's left is a foreign government trying to lead the nuclear race!

Megan decides to embark on an overnight trip, staying the night at a rustic oasis ranch, nestled deep in the canyon. I will have to admit that there's a different vibe here. After asking her peers at the laboratory, she found out that Naim was working with rare minerals from outer space. However, not those little fragments that usually arrive in comets and meteorites. These were bigger pieces that he must have received from either the government or alien sources to be used for unknown purposes. I suspect he was working on some sort of experimental weapon. I may be wrong in my assumptions.

She didn't tell anybody what she intended to do. She just took a couple of days off to proceed along the cliffs of the Inner Gorge, across the Colorado River on the Suspension Bridge, and up Bright Angel Canyon on the north side of the river to a ranch. Her cabin is furnished with bunk beds, a sink, a toilet, bedding, soap, and towels. Showers are also available. After breakfast the next morning, via the South Kaibab Trail, she goes to the trail, which provides different, yet more unforgettable, panoramic views. He was here and somebody gave him the precious load. What for? That's still a mystery. After reaching the top, she took her camera and a radiation detector to look for any clues.

As a casual tourist, she takes a mule ride around the site. The ride down is about 10½ miles (5½ hours) and the ride back up is about 7.3 miles (4½ hours). She returns to the lodge in time for dinner. I cannot be pessimistic. It was not a waste of time. I was not lucky enough to detect any radioactive material.

While Megan was not at her cabin, somebody dropped a note under the door with an anonymous message. "Wrong place, see genome." Who sent this? What's in there? I cannot fall in this setup. Megan returned to work, still thinking about the message. I will ask

Sydney just to see if she has any clues of what the message may mean.

The press conference at the space agency is about to start. Stephen runs upstairs to not be late to the event. The elevators were busy, or was it something else? I don't have time for speculation. Upon arrival, he sat next to Megan, Emmett, and Sydney. One reporter said, "What a dream team!" They didn't know what to say to that remark. Was it a compliment or just a sarcastic quip? We don't understand that kind of humor. Let it go.

The host asked the crowd, "Can consciousness be explained by quantum physics?" One of the key questions in science is how our consciousness originates. Stephen took the stage and started his dissertation. The brain's neural system forms an intricate network, and the consciousness it produces should obey the rules of quantum mechanics. Yes, the theory that determines how tiny odd particles behave. Valerie asked him, "Does this explain the mysterious complexity of human consciousness?" That's a great question. Consciousness is generated by quantum processes. Isn't it a very strange thing? The laws of quantum mechanics rule the microscopic world, or quantum-verse. They usually only apply at very low temperatures. What about quantum computers? They are currently operating at a temperature of around -272 °C. At higher temperatures, classical mechanics takes over. The human body operates at a certain temperature. Thus, any variation of the temperature of the environment must be compensated with the appropriate clothing, air conditioning, heating, and other devices to help our bodies functioning. It is expected to be ruled by the classical laws of physics. Is

that the reason why the theory of quantum consciousness has been dismissed out of hand by many scientists? Yes, indeed, there are some scientists who dislike this approach, although others are convinced supporters.
What are the principles underlying the quantum theory of consciousness? Stephen looked at Sydney, who's been working with similar issues in her current research. He replied, "They are completely unknown." What? Are you serious? Yes, I am. People started talking to each other loudly, then silence took over.
How could quantum particles move in a complex structure such as the brain? AI is assisting us in uncovering such secrets. What is that? These findings can be compared to measured activity in the brain. We are one step closer to validating or discarding the controversial theory of quantum consciousness. When are you going to do so? Soon, I promise you that.
I cannot tell anyone! What's this voice inside of me? Who's this? He keeps telling me things in a language I cannot comprehend. I should pay more attention. A deep metallic voice said, "artificial intelligence is primitive." Advanced civilizations have gotten rid of them. " Stephen replied, "Aren't you scared of it?" No, not at all. Why should I be afraid of an inferior being? Okay, who are you? Don't you know so far? No, I guess you are an alien from outer space. Whatever you say, Stephen. Wait! The voice vanished. I must be going crazy.
The main struggle of humanity today is to become more conscious and less vulnerable to the conspiracies and stupidity of senseless viral fads. That is why we speak of the fractal revolution of consciousness. Moreover, this is true whether you are

talking about humanity as a species or human society in terms of nations or communities or interpersonal relationships in a specific family or social structure or the inner mental processes of an individual human being. This same thrive for the expansion of consciousness can be seen, like a fractal, at all scales of humankind, regardless of point of view. On the global scale, humanity periodically struggles to expand consciousness beyond the distortions of ignorance and propaganda until there are situations where a critical mass of people understand what is really happening in their world and use numerical power to force an end to the oppression, exploitation, violence, and genocide exercised by those immense power structures that have been established on the planet.

On a smaller scale, there are some constraints to expanding inner consciousness by breaking the egocentric structures and subconscious habits of our minds that dictate our attention, thinking, and behavior and cause us to suffer and create suffering for others. In between those two extremes, we face conflicts and challenges to expand our consciousness in the face of abusive and unhealthy dynamics in families and interpersonal relationships; to expand consciousness in particular cultures and societies in the face of abusive wealth distribution, oppression, race relations, sex and sexuality; and to expand consciousness between nations and peoples in such a context is extremely difficult. These are barriers that humankind must overcome if it is to become at least a planetary civilization.

The expansion of consciousness is not a pleasant meditative walk in the park, for it has enemies. Within each possible level of the fractal, there are forces that oppose this expansion of consciousness. At every level, there are resistant sectors that express a tendency to keep things hidden in unconsciousness, whether it is the global power structures hiding their dehumanizing activities behind the propaganda and opacity of governments; or corporations hiding their misdeeds behind the veil of public relations; or cult leaders and religious exploiters hiding their depravity behind the curtain of doctrine and ritual; or couples and parents hiding their abuses with a cloak of emotional manipulation; or on a personal scale, the habitual subconscious mechanisms that conceal from one's own conscience the presence of a memory whose presence is disturbing. And atop all this framework is the simulation, the system that controls all the programming. Knock it off! We have science to do, and your incendiary political speech is inflaming people, at least their sensitivity.

In each recurrence of the fractal, humanity is trying to awaken from the system of falsehood by moving toward a conscious recognition of what is true. And each recurrence has its own way of preventing that movement of liberation from taking place. When we do deep inner work, we encounter the appearance of inertia, cowardice, the continual attempt to turn the mind away from what is traumatic and revealing, procrastination, fear of change and the unknown, and clinging to the comfort zone. When we fight against power structures, we end up fighting under the guise of propagandists and deceptive politicians. For every impulse toward consciousness, there is an impulse in the opposite direction coming from the darkness, no matter how big or small.

However, any expansion of consciousness on one level of the fractal helps to expand consciousness on all others. People who have expanded their consciousness internally are more adept at helping to expand the consciousness of their society because the internal manipulation of the system on an individual level is very similar to the large-scale manipulations. It is not to be ignored that enlightened people who have seen the programming and detected how the system works have disappeared.

A society that expands its consciousness in turn frees individuals to become more conscious inwardly and helps humanity as a whole to become more conscious. And any expansion of the consciousness of humanity as a whole, such as a greater appreciation of the importance of personal freedom, equality, and justice, benefits all other levels of the fractal. We just need to turn on the lights so that all that is hidden can be seen. Any new bit of light will make the whole picture much brighter, and make it much easier for people to find new light switches. That path will have to be followed until everything is illuminated, and from there, a movement toward health and harmony for our species will be inevitable.

No one can change something they are not aware of. However, once they have come to sufficient awareness, change is inevitable. The puppet show can never be mistaken for reality once the presence and will of the puppeteers have been revealed. Do you know who the puppeteer is? The light shows you the strings, and you can trace the hand that pulls them. The lights go on in our minds; what they reveal is often not pretty. Nevertheless, some clarity is coming into the world, expanding awareness of media corruption, government corruption, police militarization, xenophobia and discrimination in general. The rapid acceleration of that trend is more and more. Everything that was once hidden is now roaring into consciousness with increasing urgency. The lights come on, and the more light there is, the weaker those who try to hide the simulation, each recurrence of the fractal, become. As the lights come on, we see more and more creepy parasites that had previously been hiding in the dark. However, that's just it: we are seeing them, and when they are seen, they lose their power to pull their puppet strings from the shadows. Today I have more reason than ever to feel hopeful. It may all continue to be revealed.

Can consciousness be explained by quantum physics? I can try to do so. The neural system of the brain forms an intricate network and the consciousness it produces should obey the rules of quantum mechanics. How tiny particles like electrons move could explain the mysterious complexity of human consciousness. How could quantum particles move in a complex structure like the brain?

I must focus on my work and leave everything outside. What is the relationship between the brain and fractals? Our brains are composed of cells called neurons, and their combined activity is thought to generate consciousness. Each neuron contains microtubules. What do they do? They transport substances to different parts of the cell. What does that have to do with quantum? The theory of quantum consciousness holds that microtubules are structured in a fractal pattern that would allow quantum processes to occur. What exactly are fractals? Unfortunately, there is no simple and precise definition of fractals. Like so much else in modern science and mathematics, discussions of "fractal geometry" can quickly confuse those of us without mathematical minds. Moreover, that's a real shame, because there is deep beauty and power in the idea of fractals. Thus, let's not give up. Even though I will try to explain it in simple words. Are fractals thee-dimensional? No, fractals are structures that are neither two-dimensional nor three-dimensional. However, they have some fractional value in between. Are they those infinite mathematical patterns that are called "God's fingerprints"? They are omnipresent and it is a signature impossible to avoid. What are you telling us, Doctor Stephen? They allow people's imaginations to take place and see things. We are still at an early stage of our research to provide any further development, which may not be true after all.

Furthermore, fractals are these complex mathematical concepts that describe infinite shapes that are present in nature, in elements of curious appearance and structure, such as that of broccoli or snowflakes. Perhaps they are much more common than we all imagined and could offer a fascinating explanation of how the universe works.

In mathematics, fractals emerge as beautiful patterns that repeat infinitely, generating what is seemingly impossible. Do similar structures in our brains have a finite area? Perhaps an infinite perimeter. This may seem impossible to visualize. However, in reality, fractals occur frequently in nature. If we look closely at flowers, a cauliflower or the branches of a fern, we will see that both are formed by the same basic shape that is repeated over and over again, although at smaller and smaller scales. That is a key feature of fractals. The same is true if we look inside our own bodies. How does that work? For instance, the structure of our lungs is fractal, as are the blood vessels of the circulatory system.

What about art and fractals? Is there any connection between them? Fractals also appear in the charmingly repetitive artwork of famous artists and painters, and have been used for decades in technology, such as in antenna design. That's fascinating! All of these are examples of classical fractals, that is, fractals that are governed by the laws of classical physics rather than quantum physics.

Why are fractals linked to human consciousness? It is easy to see that fractals have been used to explain the complexity of human consciousness for numerous reasons. Moreover, fractals are infinitely intricate and allow complexity to emerge from simple patterns. They could be responsible to underpin the mysterious depths of our minds and consciousness. Nevertheless, if this is the case, it could only be occurring at the quantum level, with tiny subparticles moving in fractal patterns within the neurons of the brain. That's why our proposal is called the "quantum consciousness" theory. Does it have any chance of surviving peer-reviews and testing to confirm your findings? Only time will tell.

What do galaxies, clouds, mountain ranges, coastlines, and the human nervous system share in common? They all contain endless patterns known as fractals. They are important tools in many fields, from climate change research and the trajectory of dangerous meteorites to cancer research, helping to identify the growth of mutated cells and the creation of cartoon movies.

There are those who believe that, due to its highly complex and mysterious nature, its full potential has yet to be discovered. We are still far from unlocking its full potential.

It seems you have a gift for seeing hidden patterns in nature. What do you imply? You can see rules where the rest of us see anarchy. Furthermore, you can see form and structure, where the rest of us see only a formless mess. And, above all, you can see that a strange new kind of mathematics underpins all of nature. Megan stood up and stopped this madness. Please, knock it off. Bear in mind that Stephen is a genius and a scientist. He is above average in mind. Valerie replied, "Sorry, I didn't mean to disrespect you. That's my job to dig in to the news. "

Do you celebrate chaos as a scientist? It is not that we enjoy; on the contrary, it is a matter of science that occurs in nature. Why do you spend a lifetime searching for a simple mathematical basis for the irregular shapes of the real world? That's just your point of view. It seems wicked to pursue mathematical relationships with nature, don't you think? Of course, that's what regular people see; we spend centuries contemplating idealized shapes like straight lines or perfect circles to get beyond our civilization, to transcend progress. What's the ultimate goal of science? Science aims to explain and understand the world and the cosmos. Regardless of its potential applications, that's a tricky question. We intend to get the best for humanity. Science does not build knowledge upon knowledge just for the sake of it.

Clouds are not spheres, mountains are not cones, coastlines are not circles, and the bark of trees is not smooth, nor do rays travel in straight lines. It would have been a pity if clouds were really spheres and mountains were really cones. The chaos and irregularity of the world is what we call "roughness." It is something to celebrate.

However, our predecessors had no adequate or systematic way to describe the roughness and imperfect forms that dominate the real world. As a result, they wondered if there was something unique that defined all of nature's various shapes. Did the fluffy surfaces of clouds, the branches of trees and rivers, and the edges of coastlines share some common mathematical characteristic? As it turns out, yes. similar to itself. Think of clouds, mountains, coastlines, broccoli, and ferns; their shapes have something in common, something intuitive, accessible, and aesthetic. If you look at them closely, you will discover that their complexity is still present on a smaller scale, the quantum-verse. Underlying almost all shapes in the natural world is a mathematical principle known as self-similarity, which describes anything in which the same shape is repeated over and over again at smaller and smaller scales.

A good example is tree branches. The silhouette of a tree or a Lichtenberg figure, also known as the electron tree or also as the lightning tree, Lichtenberg figures are branched electrical discharges on the surface or inside insulating materials. Curiously similar, aren't they? They branch and branch again, repeating that simple process over and over again at smaller and smaller scales. The same branching principle applies to the structure of our lungs and to the way blood vessels are distributed throughout our bodies.

Furthermore, nature can repeat all sorts of shapes in this way. Look at the Romanesco broccoli. Its overall structure is composed of a series of cones repeated at smaller and smaller scales. The overall structure of the Romanesco broccoli is composed of a series of repeating cones. We realized that self-similarity was the basis for a whole new kind of geometry. That's what he called the fractal, and that's why it is sometimes called "God's fingerprint."

Is the end the beginning? What if you could represent that property of nature in mathematics? What if you could capture it's essence to make a drawing? What would that drawing look like? I've gained access to this incredible quantum computing power and unleashed my obsession with the mathematics of nature. Armed with a new generation of supercomputers, he began investigating a very curious and strangely simple equation that could be used to draw a very unusual shape.

One of the mathematical images of a very unusual shape comes to my mind. It is one of the most remarkable mathematical images ever discovered. It is the Mandelbrot set. This is the most advanced, cutting-edge computer-generated fractal: a swirling, feathery, seemingly organic landscape reminiscent of the natural world. However, it is completely virtual. It is infinitely complex. However, it is built from an extremely simple equation that repeats endlessly. Similarly, natural fractal shapes are constructed by simple rules, ultimately the interactions between atoms. The closer you examine this picture, the more detail you will see. Each shape within the set contains an infinite number of smaller shapes, which in turn contain an infinite number of other even smaller shapes, and so on, endlessly.

Furthermore, one of the fascinating things about the Mandelbrot set is that, if left alone, it would continue to create infinitely new patterns from the original structure, proving that something could expand forever. That's the principle for self-replicating artificial intelligence and robots.

However, all this complexity comes from an incredibly simple equation. And that forces us to rethink the relationship between simplicity and complexity. What's more, there is something in our minds that says that complexity does not arise from simplicity; that it must arise from something much more complicated. Thus, what mathematics tells us in this whole area is that very simple rules generate more complex objects. That's a big revelation. It's an amazing idea. And it seems to apply to our whole world.

There's something to keep in mind. What's that? Think about flocks of birds. Each bird obeys very simple rules. However, the group as a whole does incredibly complicated things, like avoiding obstacles and navigating the planet without a single leader or even a conscious plan. It seems like they possess a biological GPS. Some animals use echo-location while others use mustaches to detect objects. They have a very intricate biology.

Even though it is impossible to predict how it will behave. It never does exactly what it does, even in seemingly identical circumstances. Each time it executes it, the patterns are slightly different or similar. However, they are never identical. The same is true of trees. We know they will produce a certain type of pattern. Nevertheless, that doesn't mean we can predict the exact shapes because of some natural variation caused by seasons, wind, or the occasional accident, which makes them unique. Does that mean that fractal mathematics cannot be used to predict major events in chaotic systems? Yes, indeed. Although it can tell us that such events will happen, we cannot accurately foresee any timeline for them.

In addition, fractal mathematics, along with the related field of chaos theory, revealed the hidden beauty of the world and inspired scientists in many disciplines, including cosmology, medicine, engineering, and genetics, as well as artists and musicians. It showed us that the universe is fractal and inherently unpredictable.

How can fractals help us understand the universe? Besides shapes and mathematics, we are sure there's much more to them. Our team is close to bringing new evidence of their powerful connection with our bodies and consciousness. Are you talking about quantum consciousness or some sort of link between them? Quantum consciousness is a fascinating subject. It transports us to another world, a completely mind-blowing dimension. We cannot yet measure the behavior of quantum fractals in the brain if they exist. Do you think that it exists? In spite of advanced technology, which allows us to measure quantum fractals in the laboratory, we are very limited in terms of resources to get any further when it comes to the human brain. These are just baby steps in terms of its comprehension and outlining a more comprehensive approach towards quantum consciousness.

In our current research, we used a scanning tunneling microscope (STM), and we carefully arranged electrons in a fractal pattern, creating a quantum fractal. When we measured the wave function of the electrons, which describes their quantum state, we discovered that they also lived in the fractal dimension dictated by the physical pattern that we had created. What dimension is that? That's still in the works, gentlemen.

What did you use to create such an outcome? In this case, the pattern we used on the quantum scale was the Sierpiński triangle, which is a shape that is between one-dimensionality and two-dimensionality. This was an exciting finding. However, STM techniques cannot probe how quantum particles move, which would tell us more about how quantum processes might occur in the brain. We need more precise techniques that will lead us to understand the quantum level. Do you have any new techniques to achieve such refinement? We are working on the development of cutting-edge processes, including new techniques. Can you share them with us? Not at this moment. This is an experiment not proven or tested by science. Is that disappointing? Despite all this, we are one step forward and way beyond traditional science. Using state-of-the-art photonic experiments, we were able to reveal the quantum motion taking place inside fractals in unprecedented detail. We achieved this by injecting photons, those tiny particles of light, into an artificial chip painstakingly designed to form an infinitesimal Sierpiński triangle. We injected photons into the tip of the triangle and watched them propagate through its fractal structure in a process called quantum transport.

We don't construct the world as one, we do it step by step, whenever we need it. Constructs are the result of known objects being used by our brains to give us familiar images and fill the voids. Visual constructs are very common. We, in fact, do reconstruct reality; it is not an accurate depiction of what we are actually seeing. Why do we re-create reality? The idea is that a precise representation is just a survival option to fill the blanks. A hack to cope with reality that may be preventing us from getting a full image of reality. We don't have to guess. Can we distinguish reality from a simulation? You may be confused by an interphase, a higher program that is connecting the dots for you. Can you prove that? Some day we will. The only simulation I know of is one of the simplemindedness around us. Basically, mediocre people who are really dumb and think or pretend that they are smart.

Perceiving reality as it is not, is not beneficial to us. Perception is like a window to reality, while reality itself is a multiple-dimensional concrete chunk. Appearances are very deceitful. We thought that the earth was flat; it is not. We are not that blind. We have our science and technology, such as telescopes, microscopes, infrared vision, and some other instruments that help us enhance our sight and see beyond the evident reality throughout the universe.

Is space-time real? Chances are. What do you mean? It has a 50% probability that it is a simulation. Or 50% that it is real. Isn't it real? Yes, it is. Or maybe not. You can't prove this isn't a simulation. There are many coincidences and synchronicities, though. According to math, there's a limit to reality. What's that? Just to mention a few: consciousness, DNA, the speed of light, and the universe's rapid expansion.

When do you come face to-face with a glitch in the simulation, or shall I say reality? Some argue that you can see them at any time and in any place. Are they so frequent? No, not at all. Can dark energy be explained by symmetrons? The "fifth force" is undoubtedly a prospective candidate, when we talk about massive objects and dark energy. Thus, an explanation for why the expansion of the universe is accelerating at a gargantuan pace. This is a new area of science called the symmetron field. Why was it named like that? It is because it has symmetry in regions of high density, while in regions of low density, such as a vacuum, the symmetry is broken and the field mediates the new force.

Is your research taking quantum control of life's building blocks? Life, as we know it, is based on carbon. Despite its ubiquity, this important element still holds plenty of secrets, on earth and in the immense cosmos above us. For instance, astrophysicists who study interstellar clouds want to understand how the chemicals, including carbon, swirling within these nebulous aggregations of gas and dust, form the stars and planets that make up our universe and create the conditions for the origin of organic life. These interstellar clouds are cold to the extreme that it's challenging to mimic them in a laboratory. However, experts in ultracold science have tried to retreat from these conditions for several years. Do you know any of them? Yes, of course. Megan specializes in chilling atoms and molecules to their absolute limit with the help of lasers. Laser cooling techniques have advanced enormously in recently. However, physicists' typical choices of atoms and molecules don't turn up too often in everyday life.

Could you cool carbon molecules? The starting point for the laser cooling of any atom or molecule is to understand how it absorbs and emits light; that process reduces the kinetic energy of the atom or molecule, afterwards cooling it down to a near halt. Despite the necessary spectroscopic data being challenging to obtain and often requiring expensive laboratory equipment, fortunately, data for carbon molecules already existed in our database, and will soon be an open-source resource for researchers and the general public. What about molecular spectroscopy data that astrophysicists use to study the atmospheres of exoplanets? You have thought of everything. Thank you for coming. As they dismissed the audience, Stephen, Megan, and Sydney moved away from the crowd. Emmett remained in his seat, watching them go by.

Let's dive into the database and develop a scheme that should allow us to use lasers to cool carbon molecules down to extremely cold temperatures, more closely replicating those conditions within interstellar clouds. It has previously not been possible in the laboratory. Megan said, "These frozen carbon molecules may be be trapped with optical tweezers." What for? It is intended for high-precision spectroscopy. Is there any purpose beyond curiosity? Of course. There's the effort of finding their fundamental properties or ultimately for reaction experiments to study their quantum composition."

Moreover, carbon molecules are absolutely essential building blocks for so many other molecules. It's incredible to think about the possibilities of what we might be able to create with this new laser cooling method. That could include combining carbon with hydrogen atoms to study a primordial class of molecules called hydrocarbons. These carbon molecules are, in some aspects quite different from molecules that have been laser-cooled so far in labs. How come? They are amenable to the technique and also raise the possibility that more options may be on the table than we previously realized. Carbon molecules are definitely the bridge between physics esoteric molecules and chemicals.

The team is currently conducting some experiments to identify other interesting molecules that could potentially be laser-cooled. What else? It is as well pondering what other substances they could potentially add to cooled carbon for better results.

These experiments will tell how successful the carbon cooling technique will be, and they hope that their laboratory will be able to build the necessary laser setups soon. We've demonstrated that with practical applications. Moreover, this study will cement state-of-the-art technology. We just need the resources to put things together to accomplish our goals. Yes, funding is crucial to achieving them. Emmett can do the necessary lobbying to grant us such resources.

While they were talking, an explosion took place in one of the rooms next to their laboratory. People started running. They went outside, and people were running away. Stephen shouted, "What's going on?" One soldier replied, "We're under attack. Take refuge."

They managed to walk away unscathed. What a day! Are you okay, Megan? Yes, I am. What about you, Sydney? I'm fine, too. Stephen let the agency know that they were all safe and sound. Our team nonetheless seemed baffled at the recent account of events. In a fraught battle for the research, aliens are swarming the laboratory. Scientists have been fighting over the rostrum, which ended up being earned by Stephen with his new discovery. While many are hailing the outcome as a huge victory for humanity, I can't help but be amused by this unexpected interest from aliens.

VI. Quantum tunnels

A man moves in the dark, approaching the laboratory door. Once inside, he looks for something specific. He opens one drawer after another. Then Stephen noticed the strange movement in the laboratory. He shouts, "Freeze!" Who are you? The man took out a gun and aimed it at him. Don't shoot! Stephen has activated the alarm. Guards are swiftly swarming all over the area. Stephen tells the man to put it down and surrender. Nothing is going to happen to you. The man reholstered it and activated some device, then vanished into thin air. Neither Stephen nor the guards could believe their eyes. What was that? Who was he? The security chief is revising the surveillance camera videos. Let's see if we can find something useful to get our hands on him. Whoever he is, he has some alien technology unknown to us.

After all the turmoil, I have to go back to work. We've created a quantum processor that has managed to imitate nature with unprecedented precision. It even includes fractals as part of the simulation.

Speaking about quantum phenomena is not easy for most people because it is a science of the microscopic that does not follow the laws to which our eyes and senses are accustomed. Although difficult to perceive, these processes can provide humanity with a technology never seen before and, of course, unimaginable. Currently, our group of physicists who are working with Megan, led by Professor Stephen, has developed a microscopic at an atomic level, with a quantum processor to simulate the behavior of small organic molecules with surprising accuracy. For instance, the first step is to produce a fully customized drug. The result has just arrived. Let's call Sydney to join us. Some bought-off-a-sidewalk scientists are lurking around. Why is that? They smell a carcass. They are predators. Some fell-of-a-bulk-truck guys won't scare me.

A foreign government is interested in our group of physicists' work. They want to get their hands on what has been developed. What's that? It's the world's first atomic-scale quantum processor. Does the attack on the laboratory have to do with that? The security is so tight and they are not telling us anything about that incident. Reporters said, "It was carried out by aliens." Don't rule out any possibilities. Our work may have drawn the attention of beings from other worlds.

This discovery not only brings us closer to faster and more efficient quantum computers, but also enables us to create unprecedented materials thanks to our ability to mimic the behavior of molecules. This eliminates the need for quantum computers to carry long wires and operate at low temperatures like the huge systems we see today. Now we go one step further and create the first-ever quantum computer circuit at a portable size.

A man at a protest outside the general assembly shouted, "We will never understand how the world works, how nature works, unless we can begin to create it on its own scale." Sydney agreed. We conducted research and came across this discovery by chance. No, nothing happens by chance, doctor. Stephen continued, "If we can begin to understand materials at that quantum level, we will be able to design things that have never been done before." What are you thinking of, Stephen? A quantum tunneling effect! That's impossible to believe. You are trying to recreate a baby universe!

According to quantum mechanics, there's an uncertainty principle, in which a car can pass through a brick wall intact. However, since the car is a solid, massive object, the probability of that happening is negligible. Despite the fact that elementary particles are more likely to cross the barrier due to quantum tunneling, this is more so because they are not as localized as large objects, and the wave functions that characterize the probability distribution of their uncertain positions have an extended tail that can overcome obstacles.

If you hit enough tennis balls with your racket, you will find that the tunnel allows one of them to pass through the racket. Although that would require many more balls than we can jump over in the space age, it is mind-blowing.

Fortunately, fusion inside a star is made possible by the quantum tunneling effect that crosses the electrical repulsion barrier between the fused nuclei. Additionally, heavy elements such as oxygen and carbon, which are essential for life, would not form inside the star without the uncertainty principle of quantum mechanics. In short, our existence is due to quantum mechanics. Nevertheless, does tunneling also have cosmological implications? It seems that it is quintessential to all of our future interstellar journeys. If dark matter is composed of ultralight particles, those particles can move away from the sources of gravitational potential that bind them to dwarf galaxies in the Milky Way halo. In classical physics, the tidal gravity of the Milky Way can only break down dark matter particles if they are around these satellite galaxies. However, in quantum mechanics, even particles that are gravitationally bound to the nuclei of these satellites can pass through the gravitational barriers that bind them. Low-mass particles whose wave functions scatter over long distances due to the uncertainty principle are more likely to tunnel through. Is this the principle for time traveling? Space-time as one!

The popular cold dark matter paradigm predicts mass density divergence due to the so-called "spikes" at the center of all galaxies, although our observations indicate it is smoother than what we expected in terms of density. What can be done to ease the tension between theory and observation? Any suggestion will fall into the field of speculation since it has been suggested that dark matter may consist of very light particles whose uncertainty principle smooths the internal density profile of the galactic center. Because of this, the mass of dark matter particles must be of lesser magnitude, smaller than even the mass of protons. It shows that if dark matter particles had this mass, they would have emerged from potential dwarf galaxy wells in the Milky Way halo.

What's the purpose of quantum mechanics then?Quantum mechanics was developed to explain the behavior of the smallest systems known to us. Those are the elementary particles bound together by atoms. However, that universal principle can be used to study galaxies, which are some of the largest bound systems we know of. This is not surprising at all, since both small and large ones follow the same universal principles of physics. In principle, we could detect quantum tunnels in our daily lives. Some events are too rare for us to witness them. It is more like winning the lottery. We know that, in principle, it can happen, such as fusion and dark matter particles. Our constant struggle against nature is an essential part of our absurd life in the system. By allowing the creation of tunnels, quantum mechanics eliminates the need for this existential struggle. If you wait patiently, the balls will naturally fall down to the other side of the racket. Maybe we should just relax, enjoy life at the beach and leave the rest to nature. That's a simplistic and dependent vision. I'd rather go out and make things happen in a more proactive way.

Everything seems like a spiral, life keeps us falling down and around. It is an almost endless spiral until you realize that life is short, just a breath in cosmic time. Can it be a bit different from what it is? That's just your perception, or isn't it? Don't be so pessimistic and the universe will fit the pieces in front of your eyes.

What if the aliens are hostile and want to invade us? What are they looking for? They came to our laboratory, attracted by our research, perhaps the one on the fifth force. I don't think that's the reason why. What about that strange man who disappeared without a trace? He could be one of them. It is more likely that it has to do with our most recent discovery. A secret code is hidden in our DNA. What mysterious secret is hidden in our bodies? We're on the brink of finding out about it.

We have sent messages with multiple details about our civilization and even our location. It's like putting a message with a map of a treasure in a bottle and throwing it into the ocean. Someone will eventually find it at some point in the not too distant future. It is like entering a jungle and starting to scream, making a lot of noise, without knowing the reaction of the animals or possible cannibal tribes in the area.

We have raised our eyes to the sky, looking for our origins and trying to find an explanation for our world and to make contact with someone else, to know that we have some neighbors near or far, similar or completely different, intelligent or not, peaceful or violent, we don't know, we bet on something, we don't know how it could affect us. Stephen, you are very pessimistic about aliens. They are not like humans. How do you know, Megan? I don't know, I just sense it. They are watching us from their vantage point. In fact, I think they created this baby universe; they gestated the simulation with the capacity of an intergalactic civilization, or perhaps even a more developed, God-like one. Do they wonder the same thing we do?" No, I don't think so. They might have different interests and ambitions. Their knowledge about our development, way of life, resources, the asteroid belt, which has very valuable elements and minerals, the stars in our galaxy, and many other things. Like what? Genetic enhancements, development of intelligence, forms of reproduction, and experiments of all kinds. I don't like that last part. The universe may look vast on a human scale. However, it is not infinite, it is limited, and it is quite small compared to other universes in the multiverse. It is similar to thinking of the quantum world as microscopic, and probably we are the ones who are very large. The same happens with the creators of this universe. It is possible that we are in their minds. In a computer simulator, it is more plausible. Everything is a matter of perspective and relativity. If there are many civilizations of robotic beings, artificial intelligence, or very advanced beings that have devised forms of invisibility, transportation, and travel between universes and dimensions, they will not want to contact us. That is why I think that any civilization that approaches us can be opportunistic and violent with a slight technological advance. The less developed ones will not have the means to find us or travel to us.

Those who came to the laboratory can deliberately leave us a star map with a big arrow showing us their location in the cosmos, and we still can't go to visit them, not even to corroborate what their world is like, because we have neither the ships nor the technologies necessary for such an endeavor. We can't travel on intergalactic missions. We have been sending signals for so many years with our radio, television, radar, space telescopes, military broadcasts, the Internet, and other unconventional forms of communication. Do you think we have attracted them with our technological signature, Megan? It may be due to our catastrophic environmental footprint, all the space travel junk we have on the planet, thousands of useless satellites and others now obsolete and disused, created for entertainment purposes or military espionage, weaponry or attack, and only a few for scientific research purposes. Stephen replied, "Our signals cannot reach very far. For instance, at 100 light years, they would be so distorted that they could be mistaken for white noise." The CDs, DVDs, and other forms of messages used may get their attention. However, will they be able to decipher the message? Pictures don't lie; they have clear pictures of who we are and where we are located. "Pathetic" is what we are! Why do you say that? This is really foolish! It's like sending full-body nude photos to strangers on dating apps and all sorts of websites without any filter since we don't know how to specify the recipient of the message, or limit who can see it or not. Our messages may already be viral in other worlds. I hadn't thought about that.

If we are so interesting or the information we have sent is so relevant, why haven't we received a message? We've already received it! Are you crazy? It's possible. There is a fine line between genius and madness. It is unavoidable. Think of all the messages on the corn and other grain crops in the fields of different countries. Don't you find it unusual how complex some of them are and even indicate some coordinates of distant constellations? They seem to have responded to the golden disc we sent. Those messages have been so discredited that I did not give them any importance. That is exactly what the government authorities want: to downplay and hide them in order to maintain control.

Our ghost spaceships have no crew, no robots, no intelligence on board, just archaic computers for our present world. Don't forget the ETIM. What? The extraterrestrial intelligence messaging. If we continue to send messages all over the universe, someone or something is going to find us. They have already found us. They have been visiting us for quite some time, even before we had these technologies.

Friend or hostile, it doesn't matter much. This is more than just playing nice and wanting to communicate with beings from other worlds. The problem is that hostile beings respond to our messages and signals sent into deep space. What compassion would they feel for us human beings if we kill each other, fight sterile wars, and do not eliminate poverty and hunger, as well as diseases that are related to such a condition? Evolved beings will not have any feelings or emotions. If one of these warlike societies detects us, we are lost. What if we were extraterrestrials? We are not terrestrial. We can't stand the hot sun, the low temperatures of the polar areas, and we can't even swim or dive without breathing equipment, and the underwater pressure is great. We are neither fit nor adapted to this strange planet. With the most advanced technology, we would attack other planets, colonize them, and become the scourge of the galaxy. We would soon go through interstellar space, destroying and banishing civilizations from their own worlds, even bringing them to the brink of extinction! Is it part of human nature to be so destructive? Not all of us are like that. The colonization of America resulted in plunder, the extinction of many peoples, and all for the sake of a civilization that promoted its culture and imposed itself on other peoples. And there was only a difference in development of a few centuries. I don't want to think about what would happen if there were a change in the advancement of an alien civilization that considers us insignificant or disposable. With all that development, we can't expect them to have the same level of violence and belligerence as we do. You are absolutely right, Megan. We cannot, and should not, ascribe human characteristics or attributes to evolved beings so genetically and physically different from us. Neither should the way we treat the environment. We exploit it without control, instead of taking advantage of it and coexisting in a harmonious and harmless way. Who would want to visit a planet with active areas of war and a constant nuclear threat? Problems accumulate and we do not solve them by exploiting each other. We are so vulnerable. If they wanted to invade us, they would have already done so. Will we destroy ourselves before we explore the stars and colonize other worlds? We are so far away from others, so small in this world.

The Solar System is on the outskirts of the Milky Way. They prefer galaxies closer to the center of the galaxy, which have more resources. Besides that, they don't mess up with inferior, underdeveloped worlds. We have to get to a higher degree of development to get in contact with them and become part of the civilization associations.

We go down the spiral of time. They're heading our way. There's nowhere to hide and no weapons to keep them at bay. What are we going to do? Let's hope that they all come in peace to help us develop our society and not to destroy or exploit us.

Our agency has detected unusual activity in a galaxy 360 light years from ours. What's going on? Our telescopes are scanning the skies in search of an answer to what looks impossible. Can you be more specific, Sydney? I will try my best to do so. Two stars in the quadrant have vanished. What do you mean by vanished? They were thought to have disappeared into thin air. You've got to be kidding. No, I am not. Later on, hey, doctor! Yes. Please come on over here. We have some updates on the stars. They all rushed to the observatory to check on the latest details on the disappearance of those stars. Stephen approaches the lead scientist, Abby. What do you have for us? Look for yourselves. They started surveying the night sky in the direction where the stars were located. This was a binary-star system. Did they collapse? No, they didn't. They didn't blow up either. We are using the state-of-the-art telescope to get as close and clear as possible. Which one are you using? That one. Yes, that's our baby. Is it the Luvoir? No, it isn't. Neither Habx nor Lisa. Is it the Stanford telescope? No, it isn't a gravitational one. It's the Dare-X. Using the large ultraviolet optical system with laser interferometer, all the spectrum is covered. The perks of light bending granted us access to the cosmos and marked the end of the dark age.

We begin to see a spherical object and a streak between it and the sun. A spherical spacecraft is rapidly moving away from the surface of the Sun. At the same time, the streak between the object and the Sun disappears and a large shock wave propagates across the Sun's surface. I can remember it like it was yesterday. The Helioviewer is a collaborative project created to monitor our star at any time. All images in Helioviewer are obtained from space telescopes located on Earth or outside the Earth's atmosphere. The object seen in this footage is estimated to be at least tens of times the size of the Earth. The streaks seen between the object and the sun appear to indicate that the object is absorbing plasma from the sun and turning itself into fuel. It's an advanced spacecraft. A plausible reason for its existence is to collect some fuel samples. For what reason? It's not just spaceships. So what? We can speculate that it has something to do with larger structures. A Dyson sphere? It's that or something else. What exactly are you thinking about? An energy sucker! There are some other devices or beings of which we know nothing. Have we detected any technosignature that can support such claims? How far can a civilization go before it reaches a dead end? It's spooky! It certainly is. When energy is not enough to push their development, they will add more spheres and harness more stars until they get to the point that it is not sufficient to keep up their increasing pace of progress. What then? An advanced civilization can turn towards black holes to quench its thirst for energy. Of course, that's a terrifying possibility. However, what if it is just a natural phenomenon in the universe? It is not a natural phenomenon! Anything that can cause such an effect is of artificial origin. What about device failure? Some technology or experiment that went awfully wrong! No way! A weather device? There are no large objects for weather study. It's huge! Larger than us! Nothing we have is bigger than our own planet. That's true. Otherwise, it's arguably more interesting than anything we've seen in space. Interestingly, the same mystery object shown in this footage was observed multiple times four years later by various space telescopes and satellites, which captured footage of the mystery sphere. They showcase rings and a sphere-like structure. Nevertheless, part of the sphere is obscured by the sun, and the streaks of material seen in previous footage are not visible. Recently, a spherical object reappeared on the surface of the Sun. This time I could clearly see a streak of matter between the celestial body and the sun. Then you can see long streaks extending from the surface of the sun, with a white object at the far end. If you enlarge a single photo, you can see the shape of the object. No images of Earth were provided for size comparison. However, we can conclude that this object is indeed massive and considerably larger than Earth.

Our agency has contacted another solar observation project that has launched a space telescope into Earth orbit to observe the Sun. Since then, they have regularly uploaded photos of the mysterious object moving at high speed around the sun. This object appears to be butterfly-shaped. A few days later, the observatory was suddenly invaded by federal agents. The Observatory staff were shocked to receive these unannounced visitors. However, they were even more surprised when they were told that the observatory was closed due to a safety risk, and the workers were ordered to go home immediately. They didn't understand what happened, and he was told that for security reasons, the federal agency wouldn't answer any questions. A number of agents were stationed on the premises for 24-hour surveillance. A military Black Hawk helicopter was also dispatched to the scene. At a subsequent press conference, the government announced that the observatory would be closed indefinitely for safety reasons. No further explanations were given to the public, and reporters knocked on doors for answers. However, they were not that lucky; they didn't get an answer.

After several weeks, workers were finally allowed to resume work at the observatory. They did not receive any updates or real reasons for this mandatory leave. Things seemed to be back to normal. However, journalists noticed something strange.

While the solar observatory was closed, other observatories were also closed by order of the local government. Interestingly, all of these closed observatories are dedicated to solar observations. It's hard to believe that this is all just a coincidence, and it's understandable to be skeptical. For some reason, these observatories were closed for almost two weeks, and for some reason, the reason had to be kept secret from the public.

By chance, an amateur astronomer named Maria contacted her friend and former classmate, Megan. She was taking pictures of the sun at the same magical time using her own equipment. One of her pictures shows a disk-shaped object near the Sun. She took more pictures the next day. Various illuminated objects can be observed in these pictures. All these objects appear to be moving at a high speed. Maria and Megan will meet later to further discuss this weird incident.

The Solar Observatory has released a statement on the state of the Sun, noting that a large number of coronal holes have recently appeared on the Sun. Auroras occurring near Alaska were also observed for about an hour during this period. This is more than three times her normal observation time for such phenomena. From these facts, there is no doubt that solar activity changed significantly during this period when the observatory was closed. Did the government cooperate with them? I believe they were trying to cover up the anomalous activity and prevent mass hysteria. If the mysterious objects and lights seen in these videos and photographs cannot be explained by any means or natural causes, the only other possibility is that they could approach the massive, super-hot sun freely and safely. It means that it represents an advanced technology that can return to its own planet unscathed. It would be the product of a civilization far superior to ours. To them, the sun may be like a gas station, or they may refuel the sun to control the solar cycle. It's hard to believe. It is like a noble act to protect our primitive world! No, it is unthinkable. Whatever the truth may be, I'm not the only one who thinks it might be a little unwise for humanity to try to contact other civilizations in the universe with our current level of scientific knowledge.

Let's observe further. I can see something! It is kind of faint! It's there. Look at it! It's breathtaking. It didn't disappear; it just turned out to have lost its fission! How come? All we know now is that it is a faint dark spot in the night sky now, almost imperceptible to us. The other is over there, too! Where? It is where it has always been. What could have caused this? We don't have the faintest idea. We need to get closer to get more information regarding this weird phenomenon. When the top military arrived at the facilities, they came with strict orders on how to manage this issue. Emmett is also among them. He's a laughingstock. He was the first to run away from the laboratory on the day of the alien attack.

One of our telescopes is picking up some shadows moving around another star. Which one? It is in the fifth quadrant, approximately 300 light years away. It is getting closer. Let's take a look at it. As they zoomed in on the area using infrared technology, they came across some unusual activity, some kind of masking of the star. What's covering the sun? It seems to be a biological entity! What? Yes, it is. It moves swiftly around the star. Their shape is like a diamond and changes quickly into a dodecahedron. It could be an illusion. Do you think so? Everything is possible. Look at those macrotubules! Invisible in plain sight. They extend for thousands of light years. Where do they come from? There's no galaxy around. It must be some sort of artificial structure. What about a portal? Don't you think they are bringing the necessary parts to build a Dyson structure around stars to suck up their energy? That's really scary. The evidence is all over.

A Dyson sphere! That's just a theory. No, not anymore. What happens if you put a star in a large dome? For instance, if the sun is boxed in, its great source of energy would be completely controlled by such a device. Nevertheless, it won't continue to provide the earth's surface with its vital rays. Right now, just a small amount of the sun's energy reaches us. Can we use all of it? We would if we could. What's keeping us from exploiting its full potential? It's basically a technological restraint.

A few months ago, scientists flooded the media with news that a "giant alien structure" called Airawnk had been discovered around a star 1,500 light years away. Of course, we all read the sane articles. It explains that the variation in light-years of the star in question is probably due to it being surrounded by dust and comet halos. Nonsense! Can't they distinguish dust from a technosignature? I guess they are covering up the whole situation. A piece of a giant alien puzzle has been discovered as the culprit for such an amazing task. However, giant extraterrestrial structures put us in the shoes of civilizations far more advanced than we are. Imagine the problems we might face and the knowledge of astronomy and science they could have. It is an interesting concept that allows us to conceptualize them and try to solve them by pushing our frontiers.

Let us assume that human civilization will continue to develop over the next few millennia. The resources available to us are limited on the earth's surface and are being depleted by population growth, technological advances, and the increasing demand for energy. Faced with this dreary scenario, the time will come when we will have to look for alternative energy sources to avoid the collapse of our society. The sun seems to be a perfect energy source. Why not take advantage of its energy? It is the most plausible solution to our increasing energy demands. It is more a case of survival than anything else. I agree. The sun will be an excellent candidate. It radiates an enormous amount of energy 24 hours a day, 365 days a year, requires no maintenance, and will continue to shine steadily for at least another 1.1 billion years. The problem is that from Earth we will never be able to exploit its full potential: at a distance of 150 million kilometers, the surface of our planet is reached by only two-billionth of the energy that the sun emits. This does not mean that we receive too little energy; if we were to commit the folly of covering every inch of our planet with solar panels, we would have 5,000 times more energy than we produce annually. Let's do it! Hold your horses. The cost of such a project is astronomically high. Are you telling us that our

modern society can't afford to exploit the sun's energy? Not at the cost of this current technology.
Nevertheless, even that number would be too low if our civilization were sufficiently advanced. Eventually, we will be forced to devise new ways to harness the radiation produced by our star in the most efficient way possible, and what better way to do that than to build a giant hollow sphere around the sun to capture all the energy it emits? Our knowledge is zero on how to do that.
This idea has never been shared with us by future time travelers. Don't be funny, Sydney! Imagine if we could learn from this alien civilization. That would mean the biggest leap in terms of development in our civilization's history. Hey, guys! These aliens are not harnessing energy, they are pushing the limits by destroying stars, galaxies, and who knows what else to get what they want. One day, we will be like them. No, Stephen, don't say that. We are not monsters. It's a matter of survival for the fittest. You don't even know if they are biological beings or just machines with artificial intelligence that went berserk.
The concept is popular until you realize that if you get to its full capabilities, it could do more damage than good. That's also relative. From their point of view, it is on behalf of their civilization. Physicists, astronomers, mathematicians, and many other scientists are fascinated by the Dyson Sphere.
Although theoretically possible, the construction of the Dyson sphere is far beyond our technical reach. Thus, it is very difficult to imagine the details of its creation. All we can do is answer a few questions about the principles that should support such complex technology. For instance, is it really possible to place

a hollow sphere around a star? What happens in terms of gravity? In principle, this does not matter. The sphere, as a symmetrical structure, attracts the stars uniformly from all directions with the same force, so the effect of the sphere's net gravity on the stars is zero. Even if the star is not exactly centered on the Dyson sphere, it will not be attracted more in one direction than in the other. However, there is a problem with this. As it floats freely in space relative to the stars, the object that hits the structure can move the Dyson sphere. Moreover, without a system that constantly corrects the velocity to keep it constant, one of the sphere's inner walls would collide with the star, and humanity's most ambitious project would be a giant ring of junk orbiting the Sun. This will end in burning at the surface of the star. Fortunately, removing comets and asteroids from the solar system before beginning construction of the Dyson sphere avoids problems caused by other celestial bodies affecting the sphere. A Dyson sphere comet-free? Unless you design a shield to protect it from meteorites and comets, cleaning the surroundings is the best idea, even though there are too many comets in the Solar System. Such a large structure requires a large amount of material. Even if it is in the distant future, when the sun is smaller. Therefore, a Dyson sphere the size of Earth's orbit remains a rather barren giant structure. By combining the masses of all the planets, asteroids, dwarf planets, and other Kuiper belt objects in the solar system. We accumulate enough material to give the sphere about 600 kilograms of matter per square meter.
Nevertheless, there's a conjecture that we need to take into consideration. Which one? This means the

thickness of the sphere can be increased or decreased depending on factors that probably correspond to this 600 kg of material. For example, a sphere made entirely of iron would be about 8 centimeters thick. For less dense materials such as diamond, its thickness increases to 20 centimeters. In real life, planets are not a single element. However, a variety of compounds would make it more difficult to construct, unless we take whole planets and other objects in the cosmos to get the materials needed for such a structure. In other words, civilizations seeking to dismantle planets in their own planetary system must face the challenge of designing spheres using a limited number of different materials.

The force the sphere receives is another estimate that we need with surgical precision. Speaking of resistance, is there any material that can withstand the stress that the Dyson sphere receives? The Dyson sphere does not exert gravity on the star. However, the star's gravity tries to pull the sphere wall inward, creating an enormous amount of compressive force on the entire structure, which collapses into a single ring and some debris. It should be subject to change. No known material can withstand this scale of stress, even though there must be some sort of futuristic solutions that can help us reduce the stress on the structure, such as placing a large number of very large vehicles in orbit around the interior of the sphere. These centrifugal forces are transmitted to the structure against the direction of the star's gravity and escape its compression, so to speak. As a more realistic alternative, our civilization may choose to build a sphere with a very thin wall, a "Dyson bubble," which remains inflated by the radiation pressure of the star itself. Another option is to abandon the concept of continuous spheres and build a "Dyson swarm" around the stars. This is a cloud of a small collection of stations that capture energy and radiate a laser beam where it is needed elsewhere in the solar system. Despite having a problem with the latter two options, they are not solid enough to live in, just in case we decide to live in it for maintenance purposes. Can we live in a Dyson sphere? It sounds like a far-fetched idea, although it may be unnecessary due to the development of artificial intelligence and robots. Let's put it this way: The area of the inner surface of the Dyson sphere, which is the diameter of the Earth's orbit, is 600 million times that of the Earth, making it a good place to rotate.

Space problems will arise in the future. Technology is the answer to solving such urgent issues that humankind will face in the long term. We don't have that much time. Additionally, two basic requirements must be met for the interior of the sphere to be habitable: a suitable temperature and a gravity that keeps its resident's body held to the ground. A Dyson sphere of that size constantly captures all the heat emitted by the sun until it reaches a temperature of about 122 °C. On the one hand, a Dyson sphere of that size continuously traps all the heat emitted by the sun until the structure reaches a temperature of about 122 °C. In other words, without a huge cooling system, we can hardly expect an advanced civilization to live a normal life in our huge structure.

What would happen If the sphere rotates fast enough? The centrifugal force will be generated in the opposite direction to the attractive force of the central star, so the gravity problem can be solved. However, this solution creates a large amount of gravity only in the region near the equator of the high-centrifugal Dyson sphere, which adds unimaginable stress to the structure. Can extraterrestrial spheres operate in a different way? In general, it is really possible to find Dyson spheres that do not require artificial gravity or controlled temperature, among other things. Other intelligent civilizations scattered in space don't need such refinements since their biology is different to ours, and in most cases, these structures are operated by robots and artificial intelligence.

In theory, a very advanced civilization could easily build a Dyson sphere. And even more so when it does so around small stars like white dwarfs. How far would they go? I don't know. However, it's pretty cool that our scientific community has a program that scans the sky for signs of infrared radiation, suggesting that it was emitted by a hot object composed of heavy elements like this gauge structure. I think it's a realistic structure. Dash! Approximately 300,000 sources have been analyzed to date, in which 18 "weak" or "ambiguous" signals have been found that may match the expected profile of the Dyson sphere. This one is real! Could these signs indicate that we are not alone in space? It is more than obvious, even though some scientists will rather wait until we get more information regarding that structure.

Now we have some better coverage. There's a civilization nearby the star. They are fighting back. Nuclear explosions have barred some of the ramifications of the structure. This is mind-boggling. It is self-healing and self-replicating. What do you mean? It cures its wounds itself and it is multiplying rapidly. From every piece that is cut, two are coming as a response to the attackers. They are not going to hold on for long.

What can we do from here? There's nothing we can do; we neither have the capacity nor the technology to intervene in such a conflict. What may have triggered such a massive attack on that planet? Stephen blatantly said, "Simply call it energy. They need resources and they get them or else." In a matter of hours the star will run out of fuel. No, it won't. We'll see the star covered by the darkness of the veil created by the layers of the gargantuan vacuum. It will take them years to gather all the power in the star. Can we have an educated guess? We can't be more specific now. More input is needed, for instance, the speed at which they are collecting the energy. The size of the star, its stage, and other valuable details to estimate more precisely the time that it will take them to achieve such a fit. If we take into consideration what they have done to other stars, checking our galactic observations from all of our telescopes and shuttles, it is plausible that in four or five years they will have depleted that star system, and they will be moving simultaneously onto other parts of the galaxy, which gives us around 30 years to get ready before they come knocking at our door. They won't give us any signal and won't ask for permission either. They will show up and start their ferocious endeavor.

The inhabitants are subdued. The resistance was futile; now it seems they ran out of ammunition. The planet is also being sucked up by the energy-harvesting device. What will be their most likely fate? They will surely perish in such a devastating conflict against an invisible force that seems invincible. Nothing can damage it.

The puzzle is almost complete; the star is partially covered. It has taken just a few days to complete such a titanic task. The planet is on the way to being wrapped in the same darkness. There are some indications that other stars are undergoing the same destiny. The inevitable destruction!

VII. Red Alert

The world's top countries are holding emergency meetings on short notice. We should get ready to flee this world or to face the invisible enemy with all the power and knowledge that we have accumulated throughout our development. That's a good point. However, we have nowhere to go and insufficient knowledge to combat that threat. What do you suggest then? More information is needed to analyze our options. The latest update gives us a more accurate scenario of when we should expect the alien structure to arrive in our Solar System. When is that going to take place? In approximately twenty-seven years. That's not what I wanted to hear. At least we got a warning from those other galaxies.

A mysterious pact between President Howard and the aliens has finally been deciphered. Emmett combed through top-secret documents and said, "Finally, here are the classified documents." Bizarre! Aliens have had secret agreements with some of Earth's governments.

A "galactic federation" or some sort of "universal committee," seems that has been waiting for humans to reach a stage of civilization where we will understand what extraterrestrials, advance civilizations, alien technology, and advance science mean to the cosmos.

All this has sent eyebrows shooting heavenward by saying that earthlings have been in contact with extraterrestrials from a "cosmic federation" of some sort. The unidentified flying objects have asked not to publish that they are here because humankind is not ready yet for it. Aliens are being kept in hiding until humans reach at least a planetary stage.

How can you explain that Mr. Howard disappeared for twelve hours? Nobody can. A journalist came up with a story that he died of a heart attack. However, a government spokesman denied this and attributed the speculation to conspiracy theories. Mr. Howard later reappeared at a baseball stadium. Some people suggested that it was a look-alike, much like him. However, with some very subtle differences, such as the ears. The original Mr. Howard had the earlobes separate from the face, while the new Mr. Howard had the earlobes attached to the face. Unless he had a complete transplant, the prosthesis would give him a completely different smile. The new man's baldness contrasts with the thinning, almost transparent hair of the real president.

The city's airport was strangely closed to all air traffic and staff for three days when President Howard disappeared, according to the documents. Rumors began to circulate that the president had been attending a meeting with extraterrestrials at a military base on a largely uninhabited and inaccessible island in the Pacific Ocean.

In fact, President Howard actually met with two alien entourages at the time. During the first alien encounter, President Howard's plane lands on the island. Then, an alien craft landed in front of the plane, and the president boarded this spacecraft for approximately 45 minutes while another spacecraft flew over the air force base. Judging by the brief duration of this encounter, it would not be the first time this extraterrestrial group has met with President Howard.

Reports of UFO's and USO's are all over the world. What's that, Emmett? USO's are unidentified submerged objects. Sydney, I would like to tell you everything about my research. Maybe some other time. Right now, we have too many things to juggle. That's true. She hugged him goodbye. I've got to go to Congress with the evidence I collected. I am not showing this to Mr. Andrews nor Dr. Faith. This is too much for them and I don't know their involvement in this matter or some others that are even worse. I should watch my steps since I am walking on thin ice. There's so much at stake.

Emmett contacted Senator Hawthorne and handled the information that he had collected. This was preposterous. How he dared to have a pact with such beings from outer space is no longer a mystery. This is outrageous. Since you collected this data, you committed a crime. Although it was on behalf of humankind, I would like to remain anonymous, senator. I respect that. I will proceed to show the committee for alien affairs these documents. After Emmett departed, Senator Hawthorne started reading the documents, "Advanced civilizations came from Sirius B." This is more serious than I thought. It is really mystifying!

Aliens are here, sir! We welcome you, beings from other worlds, our galactic brethren. President, we are here only to prevent you from reconciling with the militant society of Proxima Centauri. Who are you and who are they? We are your ancestors from Avlast. Avlast? We don't know anything about you. We came to this place when our planet was about to collapse. The survivors split up; one group came here and the rest went to Sirius. Where did you come from? We came from Dimension 8 originally, a world four times the size of your universe. What caused your world to be destroyed? The same thing will happen to you. It is the use of mass destruction weapons by those who do not understand their cosmic reach and impact.
You did not respond. Whom are you afraid of? We do not know this feeling. This visit is of goodwill to prevent further damage. The Uitas are a pest. Whether you are with them or against them, the Uitas have no mercy. They do not recognize neutrality. We do not know them yet. There have been visits by spying sauces from alien civilizations, including yours. In fact, we have been monitoring your activity for a long time. Yes, they have. However, after we started testing the atomic bombs, and actually after the war explosions, it increased geometrically. You shot down some of our lead spacecraft in an attempt to find out what they were doing and why they were doing it. Ignorance does not justify violence. Words of wisdom, my friends of the universe. What in particular do you want from us? Lay down your arms and come to your senses so that your civilization can flourish. At present, this is not possible. Your argument is logical. However, it can't be taken into account. The president asks them to leave Earth unless you help us overcome

our current uncivilized world with better weapons and cutting-edge technology. I dismissed them when they told me that we were not ready to take advantage of such technology or progress.

Mr. President, what do you think will happen next? You must wait for the other aliens to come! There is no need to wait, his assistant told him. We have not come to an agreement with these arrogant beings. Nevertheless, we hope that a second group can be like us and come to an agreement, he said. Absolutely, Mr. President. An entourage of alien beings descended in a spacecraft onto the island shortly after the first cohort of alien visitors disappeared below the horizon. It was like synchronized choreography. They are always watching us. Yes, both groups.

We must be careful with our words and thoughts. They can read our minds. I felt the telepathy of the being I was talking to before. We still know nothing about this group. The leader of the Uitas, a grayish, thin and rather large being, came towards us. Negotiations began bluntly. What do you expect from us? We analyze your DNA and want to enhance it with ours. To avoid harming other civilizations in space, you must stop using nuclear power. Anything else? Don't negotiate with the Avlastians! And what do we get out of it? Our support. Give us advanced technology and we will be on your side. A treaty was signed for cooperation in the manufacture of interstellar spacecraft and the development of anti-gravity, anti-matter, and nuclear fusion engines.

Emmett said, "I don't have much time. I won't go into the details of this treaty." Keeping it private is our priority. Neither the public nor Congress should know about it. All right, Mr. President. Uitas disappeared before our eyes.

The details of the deal and the promises to allow human abductions by extraterrestrials for testing purposes, according to testimony at the Congressional hearings set up to investigate what really happened to the president during his disappearance, became clear. President Howard chose to ignore the Constitution and signed a treaty with extraterrestrial creatures. And we basically agreed that the aliens would take some cows, sheep, and humans to test gene transplant technology. However, they would provide details of the people involved. Unable to fight, we negotiated a kind of "surrender" with the aliens. Since they knew that we were frightened mostly by their superiority in development and technology, it was a way for us to avoid conflict.

It is revealed that the aliens tricked Mr. Howard into breaking the agreements. Aliens did not provide a complete list of human abductees and contactees to the M-12 committee, suggesting that not all abductees were brought back. We got less technology than we wanted, and it turns out that abductions exceed the millions we innocently accepted. Uitas changed their mind and started acting on their own without being bound by any treaty or agreement. This meant a breach of contract on both sides. An alien race known as the Uitas arrives on Earth in giant ships and keeps them in orbit around the planet, including spy satellites. They are also located in the deep sea and Antarctica. These safe zones were defined by treaty. The whistleblower's statement has not yet been made public. However, we have received this classified copy, which reveals that the government knew of these extraterrestrial intentions and has information on everything happening on Earth. They offered us guidance and assistance. However, we declined it. I only wanted their knowledge of advanced weaponry and technology. These aliens have offered the president to get rid of the Uitas in exchange for Mr. Howard's government destroying its nuclear weapons and abandoning the weapons development. According to several former military personnel, Mr. Howard and his team did not reach an agreement with the Avlastians. They were more interested in acquiring alien technology than in getting rid of Uitas or abandoning nuclear weapons manufacturing. Either Mr. Howard, who saw the grays' ships orbiting the planet and feared an imminent attack by them.

President Howard would have met with aliens several more times to get what was promised. Mr. Cooper, who acted as a liaison between the aliens and the government, describes what happened after the president rejected Avlastian's offer. The Grizzly is a race that hails from Orion, Zeta Reticuli, and Proxima Centauri, with different settlements. It also details the specifics of the contract signed between the government and the Uitas. The treaty states that aliens are not to interfere in our affairs, and neither are we. Their existence on Earth is kept secret. They provide us with advanced technology and help us develop our technology. They do not do business with any other country in the world. They were allowed to abduct people on a limited and regular basis for genetic testing and to track our evolution. We normally and regularly make lists of victims.

Did the fact that the treaty prohibited aliens from trading with the rest of the world mean they could only abduct humans within the agreed territory? Ship launching, reverse engineering work. The government continued to develop weapons of mass destruction.

Adams, a geotechnical engineer hired by a government-contracted company to build a subway base, claims to have been involved in a secret project regarding extraterrestrial life. During the course of these projects, he claims to have made contact with those who worked directly with these beings.

Mr. Andrews is pondering the course of action after Naim's case has been stuck for a while, and now the attention has moved towards the alien visitors and the oncoming catastrophe. Dr. Faith comes to his office. They exchange ideas on how to act against the imminent threat and the involvement of their institutions in the events to take place soon. None of them talked about Naim. They secretly know what each other's involvement was and prefer not to talk about it.

The lead detective, Johnson, was frustrated since there were no leads to solve the disappearance of Dr. Naim. The license plate didn't take us anywhere since the car had been reported as stolen. The two guys in the video have not been identified yet. They are thought to be foreigners operating in our territory. Most of them are mercenaries or terrorists. Has any group claimed to be the author of the kidnapping? No, not at all. Any sightings of UFO's in the area? Are you serious? Right now, I would take anything. There are no reports. We are back to square one. The search has been unsuccessful. He then talked to his boss and requested help. He was told, "You have nothing. People are in despair, and the government is eager to move on. This case is attracting far too much attention

and diverting attention away from our most pressing concerns. You are going to crash into a wall if you continue your current direction. Don't do that. Take a different direction, such as aliens, kidnappers, or a jealous husband." Come on!
Stephen ran into Sydney and called her out. Hey, how are you doing? I'm fine. What about you, Stephen? Megan dumped me. Oh, so bad for you! I still have you. No, you don't. Didn't we have a relationship? Are you serious? Forget about it, Stephen. I am seeing Emmett. He's a good guy, and we get along well. Alright, I wish you the very best for both of you. Don't be such a bad loser. That hit me hard, Sydney. Nevertheless, I know I will be over you sometime. As he walked away from Sydney, he faced himself alone for the first time in a long time. I must have done something wrong. Maybe too much work and I haven't paid attention to my romantic life. I deserve this.
Emmett comes to Sydney after his meeting at Congress. How did things go? I'd rather not talk about it to protect you. That bad? Yes, it is. Politicians are using their leverage to downplay things, discredit sources, and not tell people the facts. That's much of our world today. Yes, that's true. What about your code? The research is almost over, I am just confirming the results with some other samples. Sydney receives a message on her mobile phone. She shouts, "What's this?" What's wrong? The message is from an unknown number. If you want, I can track it down. Please do so. What's so disturbing about the message? Look for yourself! It says, "Fake religion, DNA, vaccines, and wasting time." Whoever sent this has some insights! No, Emmett. I have been working

very hard on this. Can you double check? We won't tell anybody about it. Espionage must be at its highest point. Even with us? Yes, indeed. We are under the spotlight, my dear.

I don't want to be a buzz kill. Why do you say that? I have a hunch that there are some weird results coming from the research so far. Like what? Somebody may have manipulated it and the code came out so easily. However, I do not share the same viewpoint. Do you get the same results with cells from other body parts? Do all individuals have the same message? Or is it restricted to a specific group of people? I don't have all the answers to all those questions. I would have to run more tests and use different criteria. Who provided you with the samples? Dr. Faith did. Get your samples and run the tests as soon as possible. This smells fishy!

On second thoughts, they decided to do something different thereafter. That doesn't seem logical enough. Detective Johnson wanted to dig a little bit more into what connection there must have been between the religious leaders and the disappearance of the young scientist. He was too honest about his feelings, and that was a red flag to his boss, who immediately dismissed the idea of further investigating such an influential figure without any evidence or indication that he had some involvement in the case. However, this is clearly an attempt to discredit Johnson's investigation alone, highlighting the loopholes that the case already has, and it would be almost impossible to proceed at a legal level. I know that I can make him spill the beans. All I need is a few minutes and he will break.

The government keeps its narrative of a red alert even without a certainty of what is going to happen. Nobody knows for sure. Anybody conspiring against its interests will face the consequences. That seems unremarkable.

Even though there's no silver lightning at the end of the road, most countries' arsenals are ready for the threat that is coming to our planet. We are not capable of timely sending one attack to the nearest star to prevent Airawnk from coming. Our technology is very rudimentary and we cannot achieve the speed of light. Consequently, we shouldn't dream of exceeding it at this very moment of fear. The general assembly has gathered the security council with only one purpose: to evaluate the weapons that are available for the world to at least try to stop the alien attackers. They agreed that the weapons do not need to be in one single country. They will be shot from different locations. So far, 100,000 nuclear bombs and missiles are ready to be launched at the sun as soon as we detect an alien presence in its vicinity. It was also recognized that the extraordinary effort that the international community has displayed to create a spacecraft with the technology and weapons to get as close as possible to the target before any massive nuclear attack. The leading scientist, Dr. Stephen, is present at the meeting. He says, "We are not going to make promises." We already have the spacecraft that will take us there; it is propelled by nuclear fusion; and we also have a card under our sleeve. " A secret weapon? Yes, gentlemen. Can you at least give us more details? We may do so later on when everything is ready and done. Many ambassadors were infuriated by the scientist's words. How could he keep it secret?

We need to know everything now. Please, calm down! This is not a competition among our nations. It is a united effort against one common enemy. The session is adjourned until tomorrow. What for? Are you coming back to give us further details? If my president authorizes it, I will. That triggered an avalanche of calls to their own governments and from there to leverage their forces to get the weapon unveiled.

Stephen smirked and said, "I just dropped the bomb and they naively fell for it. I have to rush to the test site for the final adjustments to the spaceship. I hope that the rest of the team has finished testing the lasers because that's basically all we can offer. Little did they know."

Due to the threatening nature of the Airawnk approach, no resolutions have been made yet. Although there may have been pressing issues to discuss, everything has been wiped off the table due to the imminent alien invasion. The evidence of the hostile nature of these extra-terrestrial creatures has given rise to claims that they are voracious and invincible. These aliens are destroying galaxies and stars and will soon be around us. Some people still think that this conundrum is a made-up issue that isn't real. Many conspiracy theories are on the move. However, when reality hits us hard, there's nothing else to believe.

Regardless of the viability of this alliance, every country in the assembly room has promised their entire nation's forces are ready to fight against the aliens with what they have available. Long-range ballistic missiles are being deployed and countries are making the necessary arrangements prior to the beginning of the confrontation.

Aliens are already in our galaxy, and it is not surprising that they are being met with the utmost hostility wherever they go. No prior civilization was successful in hurting them. No damage at all was achieved. Peace efforts are futile now. Currently, the aliens are unavailable for communication. And for the time being, humans are all trying to form military bonds with one another and, in turn, defeat the aliens. It emerged that the security council was set to appoint astrophysicist Morton to lead international efforts to respond to visitors from outer space. Although Dr. Stephen was also proposed for such a position, he didn't get enough votes. Stephen said, "It doesn't matter; I won't be here for long. My destiny is sealed."
The assembly's Office for Outer Space Affairs has been trying to contact the alien beings to negotiate with them. It sounds really cool. However, Dr. Morton has denied the supposed contact. He said, "We haven't been able to get in touch with them." It seems that either they don't understand us or they deliberately ignore us."
When the inevitable alien invasion occurs, it will be loud, violent, and highly offensive to most of us. And they will show no remorse for humanity.
After the diplomatic missions began requesting more transparency from our government, the president decided to show them what we have developed to protect our beloved planet. It was announced that in tomorrow's meeting, a thorough explanation will be part of the presentation at the security council.
Governments have agreed to pause wars to fight against the extraterrestrial menace. Even though we don't know for sure if these alien creatures are trying to take over the planet, there's something that is

unarguably imminent: the destruction of our star and our beloved planet.

While the boffins get their tentacles in a twist over who is in charge of alien contact on Earth, it is the leaders of big countries, not the international agencies, who are going to have the final say on what is going to be said the general population. Who is going to say that? That's already established by the most powerful nations.

VIII. The Code of Codes

With all the commotion caused by the Dyson sphere, they have completely forgotten about the code in our DNA. However, I am pretty sure that as soon as the matter settles down, they will come at me asking for results. I'd better get going to finish this thing quickly if it can be decoded at all.

The human body emits a glow, a light that is one thousand times less intense than the levels of regular light that we can see with the naked eyes. All living creatures emit a weak light, a faint light that can be seen through very sensitive cameras. The body's glow goes up and down during the day, being the lowest at 10 am. and its peak at 4 pm. It suggests that there's light emission linked to our body clock, metabolic rhythms, and circadian rhythm. It is assumed that faces glow more than the rest of the body. It is due to stress and receiving more sunlight. Our DNA contains valuable information regarding our life energy and "aura." What energy propels such emissions? Life itself, hence, has an impact on our health. The DNA inside each cell in your body vibrates at a certain frequency. Which one? It's several billion hertz. That's mind-boggling. It's exactly the same frequency at which modern smart phones work. It is the result of the coil-like contraction and expansion of our DNA several billion times per second, and every time it occurs, it squeezes out one single photon, a biophoton, a light particle in a living organism. It contains data about what's going on in your DNA. One single biophoton has four megabytes of information. Correction! It has four pentaquarks! There's no question whatsoever this is the era of quantum mechanics. I could be totally naive if I think that your government would share such breakthroughs with the whole world. That's very unlikely.

Furthermore, it relays this information to other biophotons in a field outside the body. As all the biophotons communicate with each other bidirectionally, they create an aura that surrounds our body. It regulates the enzymes. The data is sent back to your tubulin, your connective tissue. These impulses at the speed of light translate into activating or deactivating metabolic functions at the cell level. We are light beings seeking to transcend and become enlightened. What for? We deserve to see reality as it is, without any filters or fillings.

Since the ancient Hebrews also used the alphabet as a number system, each letter corresponds to a sequence of numbers. Over time, many different approaches have been taken to uncover an underlying code in these sacred books. What is the number of God's name? One of the last principles is unique divinity. Absolute transcendence of one as the primary source of information:

It is for everything to exist. "Everything is power. If it does not.

There is no existence, there is nothing, there is no essence, there is no intellect, there is no first life radiated by man. Human duality is in our DNA. The hyperfield, the unconscious, and collective consciousness are all interconnected. This unique identification drives our lives to seek false paradigms and false goals. Each is part of the whole, and the whole is part of each other. From a quantum perspective, atoms are 99% vacuum; the rest are unstable sub-particles of energy and pure probability. All the matter that makes up our bodies, planets, galaxies, and the universe is intertwined. We share the same elements. However, we represent less than 5% of all the matter that exists in the universe. Subtract dark matter and dark energy. We are all part of the same field. We share waves and vibrations of a certain frequency. Each of us is unique, a differentiated expression of the same elements. Nevertheless, with the same frequencies in organs such as the heart, brain, etc. We are not separated from each other; collective consciousness connects us. We are all part of it. Furthermore, we are never completely separate. The past, present, and future are all here. We all come from the same primordial matter, quantum field, divine matrix, grid, or divinity.

Consciousness is another form of matter. Matter is not the origin of consciousness; on the contrary, consciousness is the substance in which matter expresses itself. Do we live in an illusion or a simulation? This universe is the result of a master plan, not a random or sporadic result. We are not individual beings. Moreover, we are not all in this farce. The enlightened, the awakened to reality, question all programming and its constant loopholes, full of repetition and patterns. They live, knowing how reality works. They are catalysts to change the collective unconscious.

This research has been a roller coaster, from huge flops to this sweet exuberance. Translating and then decoding should be our priority. I've picked some of the key areas to keep an eye on when to this sweet exuberance. Translating and then decoding should be our priority. I've picked some of the key areas to keep an eye on when searching for the code of codes in our DNA. There's a numerical sequence we have to highlight, making an extraordinary effort to get to the bottom of it. Thus, it is fair to think that we are close to the big one. These agonizing hours are incredibly exasperating. We have been capable of getting to this point. We can surely take it to the end. We should leave any earlier disappointment behind. Right ahead is the prize awaiting to be discovered.

This is a unique opportunity. The upshot of that is the fact of facing reality with not having time to finish the research appropriately. Rushing is inevitable due to time constraints. Some heavy downpours and thunderstorms won't allow me to use outdoor facilities. If the weather improves later on, I will take advantage of sunlight to reflect the text with a quantum lens and see the complete text in detail.

Seemingly out of nowhere, a "wonder spaceship" swooped down on the laboratory, blindsiding Sydney. What's that? They are here. They are coming! Who are they? The aliens. What are they after? They are coming for the code, that's obvious.

Scientists discovered that some genes appeared to lack data, purpose, or a clear function. They call them trash genes. They knew little, and they would be in for a huge surprise. Everything makes sense, at least with a purpose.

Sydney said, "Finally, something really valuable. I was stuck on the names, numbers, and codes." What came out of the quantum computer analyses was fascinating, although it didn't bring out any clues on where can we use the code. The trash genes definitely have some inherited information from our ancestors regarding our behavior, beliefs, and attitudes. That's why some children have their grandparents' personalities or some distant relative that the child in question never met or heard about until recently. That's due in most cases to the fact that this person may have died before the birth of that particular child. Is this some kind of conditioned information from our ancestors? Some sort of karma. Here it says how we can overcome it. What is that? By transcending. What about reprogramming yourself? Getting out of the system. No, just knowing the system. The next code is, "How to change reality from the quantum realm?" It is not so clear how we can achieve that.

Mathematics' little dark secret! What's that? God's a number! Are you talking about the golden ratio? No, not all. Then what is it? Souls reincarnate in crops. That's an old notion. Nothing fancy, my dear. Number 10! It is perfect! A divine number generated by the divinity. It means profound pure unity and it begets the mother of all things, comprising all bounding, swirling consciousness, a holy ten. It is the most sacred. We have ten fingers, ten toes, The tetrax with ten symbols, the pinnacle of numbers. There have been other numbers considered as well in the past, such as seven, eight, three, nine, and eighteen, among others. What about all mighty number one? It is both even and odd, undividable, the cosmic calm that created the chaos in the universe, oneself, the number one in competitions, and so on.

After living in the system all of your life, you need to unlearn and relearn to get rid of the old program. Rewire your brain, create new synapses, and become anew. You learn more about yourself in the process. Let go of the things that are not useful to you. What you need is inside you not outside. Be in the present and aware.

We are born in this vast cosmos with a provided template of behavior and programming. Humankind is close to a huge breakthrough. Our soul's journey is written on our DNA. Is it the same for everyone? No, it varies from one individual to the other. "Conscious creator code?"

Sacred Codes? They have revealed all the knowledge of the universe. How can we activate them to fulfill our desires? Based on mystical mathematics, this series of numbers represents the "Age of Change." They move the energy that helps the universe. There are divine rules that promote the prosperity and happiness of humanity. They provide us with invaluable knowledge.

They are not just numbers. The Sacred Codes represent magical combinations that put universal energies into action. When channeled and repeated in the right way, they open portals that have long been closed to humanity. In this way, they can reach distant galaxies, contact other civilizations, and help them achieve goals and desires that would otherwise be unattainable.

Some code that works very fast. Others take a little longer. Perhaps because we are not yet ready for what they can offer us, we must work patiently and fearlessly to overcome the quantum blocks they have. When the Divine Codes are activated, our own energies merge with the energies of the "Beings of Light" that lead us to a "Manifestation," the "Cosmic Collective Consciousness" that gives us what we seek. Of course, they must be activated from the heart and have full confidence in their power, with benevolent intentions for humanity so as not to harm others. We have to reach the right vibration. The Scriptures are an urgent resource, and in addition to the knowledge they provide us for material and technological development, they are still available today. Corresponding to the mathematics of another dimension. They are basically numbers that move certain energies. When a sacred code is activated, the energy of the person using it merges with the light as a result of manifestation. In other words, it opens the door to transcendence.

Sydney wants to activate the divine code of numbers in our DNA. She needs to understand that this is a resource that you must trust with all your soul. These codes belong to the "Heart Realm" and only work for those who vibrate in this order. Before I share with you some important secrets and all the knowledge of the universe. We have sacred codes that allow you to achieve our goals. We need to know how to use them properly. How do you decide the right time and the right place? I need to concentrate and put all the energy in my heart into reciting the code and trusting it completely. The best thing to do is to find a place where you can be alone for a while and find a place that feels good. It has to be a very special moment. Add something to help you concentrate, such as candles, incense sticks, or relaxing music. It's time to activate your code. Yes, activate the code when everything is ready. So that you don't get lost while I speak the sacred code, I use a 45-bead necklace or 45-knot string that serves this function. It is a metaphysical ritual, even if you think you shouldn't do it!

I recite the scripture on the first bead, repeat it twice, and move on to the second bead. So to the end of the thread. When you prepare an affirmative prayer, you give the code one way. "God's justice protects me," "Angels are my guardians." Nothing happens.

You can say the code in your head or with your voice. It is important to feel the vibration this number creates in my soul. It may be easier to say it out loud at first. You can recite the numbers that are most convenient for you. For example, the number 123 can be said 123 at a time or count: 1, 2, 3, and so. Moreover, for longer numbers, you can say 2 twice or 3 thrice. It is important that it comes from the soul. After reciting the sacred code, it is important to thank the Divine for allowing us to vibrate at this frequency. Once you find this code, keep it in mind and use it whenever you need grace and guidance in your life. These rules apply universally to all humanity.

IX. Airawnk

Airawnk is getting closer to the Solar System. When exactly is it coming for us? We estimate that in a month or two it will be passing the Oort cloud and approaching the dwarf planets past Pluto. That's not too much time. Is there any idea when it will get close to Earth? It may be in approximately six months.

What do we have to face it? Basically, nothing. We haven't created any defense against the alien threat. Let's have an emergency meeting with the most brilliant scientists on the planet to brainstorm the course of action. We have no time to waste. It seems that's precisely what we've done over the years. What do you mean? We've been warned of their presence and their activity. However, what has been done? You're right. It has to do with our technological development. We have no device to match theirs. It's time to improvise.

Sydney has the code and it is time for the president to authorize the use of the knowledge it grants humankind.

The Avlastians return to Earth. As they met Earthling leaders, they looked at the day sky and said, "All the magnificent world you have wasted has come to a halt." Can you help us face Airawnk? There's time for everything. You don't seem to quite comprehend this moment. What are we missing? They have never been stopped! Nobody knows how to destroy them. Are there many? No, they aren't. How can we avoid our destruction? If you don't want to perish, you should run away, into deep space or even farther. Where to? To another dimension, universe, or realm. We don't know of any technology or means of traveling to such places. What about you? We do. However, we are not sure that you deserve to continue living somewhere else.

The universe is someone else's mind and we live in it. Is this a simulation? You know the answer to that question. Your scientists have already unveiled the secrets of the cosmos. It sounds like you're going insane. Nevertheless, there is some evidence to prove it. These were obtained during Dr. Stephen's research conducted a few years ago. Look at this! A red-stained neuron from someone's brain. Is that another neuron? No, it isn't. Then what is that? It is from a computer simulation of the universe, showing a structure called the "cosmic web." What is a cosmic web? You might think of the universe as a vacuum with very little matter. In fact, gravity forms threads of matter between galaxies made up of matter and dark matter found throughout the universe. These "strings," along with countless galaxies, form a huge network throughout the universe. Researchers compared this image of the cosmic web to a neural network formed from brain cells. As you have noticed, the structure of the brain and the universe are alike. However, this alone does not mean that the universe and the brain are structurally similar. Humans are naturally very good at finding similarities between different things. For example, if you look at cracks in the walls or clouds in the sky, you will start to see the outlines of animals. This is because our brains tend to look for similarities quickly. Just because brain cells and images of the universe are similar doesn't mean their structures are actually similar.

However, the neural network of our brain resembles the cosmic cosmic network in every way: structurally, morphologically, and in terms of network properties and memory capacity. The results of a quantitative comparison of human brain cells and cosmic web simulations are therefore very reliable. The human brain contains 86 billion nerve cells and the neural networks formed by these cells. In contrast, our observable universe contains a cosmic web of about 100 billion galaxies. Some similarities were found in the structures of both networks. For instance, the densest and thinnest parts of a neural network in the brain differ by a factor of exactly 100, or 1 μm per 100 μm.

Shockingly, the same range of densities has been observed in space. The densest and least dense parts of the cosmic network are also 100 times different than 500 million light-years, or 5 million light-years apart. This degree of similarity is rarely observed in nature between the structures of different objects with mesh patterns. If we looked at the nodes of the brain's neural network compared to the nodes of the cosmic network, we couldn't tell them apart. Their analysis showed four to five axons extending from each neuronal node and about four galaxies connected to each node of the cosmic web.

More interestingly, by using the entire network of the cosmic web for information storage, about 4.3 petabytes of information can be stored. In contrast, the human brain can theoretically store 2.5 petabytes of information. 4.3 petabytes and 2.5 petabytes seem like a lot at first. Your data is reliable, even though you should use other units, such as quantum units. Furthermore, small differences in the structure of neural networks in the brain can lead to exponential differences in the amount of information they can store. It is as if the cosmic web is a structure designed to store the amount of information that intelligent beings like humans accumulate over their lifetimes.

Additionally, water makes up 77% of the brain's mass and dark energy makes up 70% of the mass of the universe. There are many other similarities as well. The fact that the human brain is so similar to the universe seems to suggest something deeper. What is

that? I would like to express my own opinion. However, it would be speculation. Myths and legends have been passed down over the years in many civilizations around the universe.
"The universe is born from the body of a "divinity" and has its own consciousness." Although they all come from different legends, they tell the same story. We live in the body of a "god." Looking at these stories from a modern perspective, we might think that they are nothing more than the primitive beliefs of our ancestors. How wrong we have been. What if the universe was self-aware? What if it is conscious? Or is it a giant brain? What does science say about this? Let's look at the evidence and try to deduce how it's actually true. We humans are part of the universe. Since we are conscious, the universe is conscious through us. This is the standard short answer to the question, "Is the universe conscious?" It might be conscious. However, can the universe have a consciousness separate from us and other conscious beings? This concept has a name. It's called Panpsychism. It is an essential aspect of many religions. In fact, in some religions, there is nothing but consciousness. If you embrace panpsychism, then the universe works not only with our consciousness but also with its own consciousness. So is it true? First, we must decide what consciousness is. Some neuroscientists and psychiatrists have proposed a way to measure how conscious something is. They propose that consciousness has to do with how much control a being has over itself and other things around it. This theory separates intelligence from consciousness. These are two different things. For instance, a highly intelligent quantum supercomputer could routinely

think better than humans and beat humans in chess or dangerous situations. Nevertheless, it would have no will of its own. A programmer controls it. Therefore, intelligence and consciousness are two different things. A being does not have to be highly intelligent to be conscious. Based on this idea, we can say that trees are more conscious than rocks. Earthworms are more conscious than trees. Cats are more conscientious than earthworms. Humans are more intelligent than cats. And the ultimate consciousness may be the universe itself. If consciousness works this way, the complexity of an organism's brain is related to its level of consciousness. And scientists actually have good evidence that everything has some sort of consciousness. Even those without a brain? That's something that still has to be proven.

Consciousness is a cosmic web that seems to be interconnected and communicating with other systems. Neurons can be triggered by specific stimuli and send signals to each other. And a large and complex network of these neurons seems to emerge in consciousness. The more complex the network, the more consciously something appears. Is there evidence of such a "brain" or network of connections in the universe? There is a huge network of galaxies in the universe, with hundreds of billions of galaxies. This is the same network of billions of interconnected neurons in the brain.

The difference is that each of our brain cells can send signals to, or at least fire, other brain cells. Do galaxies have such communication mechanisms between them? Apparently not. However, we must remember that almost all galaxies have a black hole at their center. It is like the nucleus of a brain cell. What Happens in a black hole? We don't know because the equation collapses at the singularity at the center of the black hole. That is the point where time and space cease to exist and equations cease to work. Is it possible that something is going on here that we just don't know about? Black holes could resemble brain cells only if they were somehow connected and able to send signals to each other. It behaves like a giant information processing device. However, it is actually intelligent, possibly even conscious. This is like a superconsciousness that can theoretically control not only the universe, but also time and space itself.

Nevertheless, I think I'm getting too excited about the possibility of speculation entirely. In other words, does what we see around us require consciousness to bring to life the events that led to what we observe? If the universe were completely unconscious, what we see now would be different. Or perhaps not much.

There is no evidence that consciousness is necessary to orchestrate the events that led to its current state. Science allows evolution to occur naturally over long periods of time without the need for a conductor. What is the beginning of time? Did consciousness guide the Big Bang? This cannot be ruled out. Consciousness may be involved. Nevertheless, to attribute this event, without evidence, as divinely inspired by cosmic consciousness is absurd. It is as speculative as saying it was caused by as yet undiscovered laws of physics. Furthermore, after the Big Bang, there is no evidence that anything was consciously controlled, as the events can be largely explained by the laws of physics as we know them. The universe has other laws that do not relate to what we know of our current science. And these laws do not require recognition to be enforced.

Neuroscientists believe that organisms are conscious because they can change their behavior to adapt to new situations when they are approached. They consider this a way to measure an organism's level of consciousness. Even trees have consciousness because they change their behavior, such as dropping leaves in winter or fighting disease. Given this metric, can our universe be considered conscious? The universe does not appear to change course under any circumstances. The laws of physics are supposed to be uniform throughout the observable universe. Although it is not proven science, no deviations from these laws have ever been observed until now. Yes, there are things we don't yet understand, such as dark matter and dark energy. However, they are uniform everywhere they exist and behave in a predictable manner. If the universe makes a decision, we may see unpredictable changes in the behavior of the universe that can only be explained by conscious decision makers. Then what explains the cosmic fine-tuning? For instance, the gravitational constant is as accurate as it is, and other laws such as entropy and gravity are so large that stars form galaxies, and star remnants form planets. formed. And on these planets, complex molecules are formed whose interactions may over time result in intelligent beings with consciousness as the ultimate result. This is just a coincidence. Or is it something deeper, perhaps a product of some sort of consciousness that permeates the universe and gives it meaning? A panpsychist would argue that the conscious universe established these laws from the moment of creation to maximize their worth.

Materialists believe that if there are enough universes in the multiverse and given enough time, a universe like ours in which conscious intelligent beings can evolve is inevitable. I would argue no.

"Was our universe made in a laboratory by a divine being and implanted in his brain?" It is written in your cells. Where? Our DNA. It would be dismissed as nonsense by other leaders and many scientists. Sydney got a lot of attention because she has written her final report on such research. She claims that all the knowledge of the universe is embedded in our DNA, besides God's name and instructions, our mission in life and beyond it. You have all the answers in your hands. We should revise that data right away!

What kind of intelligence do you think exists in the universe? Intelligent life in our universe can be categorized into four types. Class A lives are at the highest tier and can create other lives, either biological, synthetic, or artificial. While class B organisms are incapable of generating life. However, these organisms can alter their natural environment. For instance, they can modify planets and make them habitable. In regards to class C life, they can only partially alter the natural environment. If a planet is inhabited by these creatures, it changes radically. In addition, they will face extinction at some point in their existence. Modern humans are classified as the class C. Finally, class D beings are just as intelligent as class C beings. However, through evolution or involution, going in the wrong direction of development, they eventually face self-destruction.

Avlastians believe that the existing and dominant beings of Class A created Class B and the lower classes. They also predict that if humans continue on their current path, they will fall from class C to class D. Moreover, their leader tells us about the reason why humans cannot meet other intelligent life forms in the universe. The universe, including our planet, was created by a Class A being using "quantum tunneling," and it is what is called a "baby universe." What about your civilization? We are from a different universe. However, we must share the same origin and path. Even you are not sure about it. Nobody has faced Class A beings and lived to tell.

It is known that humans belong to class C and exist in a different universe than class A. It might be easier to understand. We are in a laboratory created by a class A being. If Professor Stephen's "laboratory theory" is correct, we cannot deny the possibility that this "laboratory" itself is some kind of organism. Avlastians agree that for the first time, human scientists are on the right track to understanding the cosmos. Two Avlastians accompany Megan, Sydney, Stephen, and Emmett to the lowest level of the base, where the code is kept secretly in a vault. We are going to share the knowledge of the cosmos with you in the hope that together we can find a solution to the attack of the Airawnk and save our world. What's at stake is bigger than what you can imagine, humans! If we find a way to stop them, then this universe and other dimensions will be safe for the first time in a long time. They are like viruses that spread and destroy everything.

It is unknown if the creator itself is a Class A being. At least it can explain why the universe and the brain are so similar in structure. Just an aside moment here. It should be easy to understand what the existence of a class A, B, or C would be like. However, what about the existence of class D? I've thought about it a lot. I think D-class beings are similar to the "Asuras." They live in the "Asura realm" and have many amazing abilities. However, they are very morally degenerate, extremely passionate, belligerent, and willing to do anything to achieve their goals. It seems that modern humanity has begun to fall into the realm of the Asuras, doesn't it? We have thrived by evolving. However, there are still many people that are taken by involution and are pushing our society towards a retrograde world of anarchy and darkness. Even so, science and technology have given us many wonderful abilities. Despite the fact that we have sacrificed the natural environment in order to evolve. And we have sacrificed countless lives to accomplish our goals. We are ruled by endless greed that seems to be dragging entire societies into a bleak future.

I don't understand why Professor Stephen claims that you can fall from C-class to D-class. Let me explain it to you, Megan. I believe it can really happen if we don't think a little bit more about our future as we grow up, the use of technology, artificial intelligence, weapons, and most of all, the role of humans in this new world. Those are words of wisdom, humans!

Let's get back to the code. That's our main focus now. Based on Avlastian's knowledge and hypothesis, I would like to reconsider the relationship between the universe and dark energy. Sydney remarked, "We have no time for theoretical exercises." The threat is knocking at our door." We all know that. Even if this is a long shot, it is the only feasible option we have to respond to that menace. The only way this can fail is if we don't understand the code. That's exactly why we want Avlastians involved in the application of the sacred number, the divinity itself.

Imagine the following experiment: intelligent beings living in our brains. What would it look like for these beings? You shouldn't take into consideration viruses, microbes, parasites, or any non-intelligent life. Of course! You can also observe neurons and neural networks. Where are you taking us? If we inhabit a brain, and they are similar to a virus or some sort of microscopic being, there should be a way of dealing with them. Don't send white cells to kill them. We might as well perish in the attempt. That's exactly why we are pondering the options and the odds of succeeding. Humans, focus! We have the knowledge, just present it to us! Megan reacted, "Why are you so eager to see the code?" Sydney also remarked, "Your attitude is suspicious. Who can guarantee us that you didn't send Airawnk to us?" Stephen intervened to settle matters down. We have no choice but to trust them by now. The Avlatians' leader said, "Your point is valid. Whoever gets the chance to have the code could conquer the universe and its effects would be devastating to all living beings in the cosmos." Something tells me that you act in a goodwill manner without malice. That's why I still want to believe there's hope for this world.

They opened the vault, and the code was in a small crystal. Where's the code? It is in our DNA. Among humans only? We don't know. If we want to find out about yours, we should take some samples from you and give it a try. The Avlastians agreed to get the answer to the universal question. Who holds the key to the cosmos? Sydney rushes to take the samples and analyze them at the laboratory upstairs. They bring the crystal to the quantum computer at the back of her laboratory. She started running the DNA test, and she showed the alien DNA on a big screen on the wall. It's fascinating, Megan said. We have never worked together like this. Yes, so united and toward a common pressing matter that is threatening to extinguish our species and probably the whole universe. Things will never be the same, at least as we know it.

Since we don't have the sequence of your genome, it is going to take a couple more minutes. The numbers came out quickly. You! Avlastians have a different combination. Will it work the same? We have to test it! Stephen shouted, "It is different for one reason." Which one? There's no code at all! It is all a hoax. Avlastians didn't reply to Stephen's claim. Moreover, Avlastine, his leader, handled them another crystal. Megan managed to run it on their quantum computer. Can you translate for us? Sure, my pleasure. As Avlastine decoded the message on the crystal, it was a menu to choose your language! Stephen steps in again. It seems it is the missing the knowledge we urged to the cosmos! How do you know, Sydney inquired? Let's see what information we can use for our most pressing issues. There' nothing worst than the alien threat on the Dyson sphere.

Look at the sequence! They didn't coincide in the end. No. They are out of this world. As they continued, they had access to the endless data base of the cosmos. This is the largest library of the multiverse.

The Avlastians said, "We are all aliens in our own land. We've all endeavored on long journeys throughout the cosmos in search of a place we could call home." Sydney said, "Water is clear and can be found all over the brain." We literally swim through the water. However, we cannot be observed.

Megan shows us a satellite image of the creature. It looks like a plant, and its leaves are covering that star. No, don't be confused by its mutating abilities. It appears to me that it is a squid. Those arms are replicating and covering all the surface. Is it a plant or an animal? It could be both. Its genetics is unknown to us. Can we communicate with it? We haven't had any success at trying so.

If we can get out there in deep space, we may be able to solve the mystery of Airawnk. Also, consider how similar the network of structures in the brain and the universe are. Don't you think that the brain and the universe work in the same way? For instance, two molecules of the same structure also have similar properties. When pharmaceutical companies develop new drugs, these properties are used to assess drug toxicity. I know where you're going with that claim, Megan. We can infect or, better yet, use some huge antibiotics to target the creature. That's not so easy, my friends. The code has granted us access to privileged knowledge. In a few minutes those doubts will vanish.

Any similarity or correlation between these structures and functions can be seen in other examples. If there exists a correlation between the brain and the universe, it is highly likely that consciousness like ours exists in the universe as well. It actually does. We have acknowledged a collective consciousness of all beings, dead or alive; all matter and dust particles, and subparticles; all the individuals and all the realms, dimensions, and universes are intrinsically intertwined in this cosmic web of consciousness. It is

the biggest network in the cosmos. They network is constantly exchanging and sending information to each other, much like the nerve cells in our brain. So, are things conscious? To some extent.
Megan said, "Modern science is becoming more and more open to the unexpected, and what may have been hindering scientific progress is over now." The code has opened new possibilities. Maybe we're trying to see beyond our eyes. It is time to receive the database! Stephen, the leader of the Avlastians, Avlastine shows them a diagram that will provide them a means of propulsion faster than the speed of light as shown on the screen. Emmett said, "The computer won't support such speed or the amount of data." Stephen asks the computer to slow down to a human pace to interact with the alien crystal. Can we do that? It immediately simmers down. He asked, "How can we get rid of Airawnk and save our world?" The screen is showing some instructions with some strange symbols. The Avlastians take advantage of the confusion and grab the crystal back, swiftly disappearing in thin air. Where did they go? They fooled us! What did they want? It was the code. Sydney added. It is useless to them without the key. What key? A password that Sydney uncovered! It is worthless. They are superintelligent and they know better. They will find out about it sooner or later. Sydney says, "That's irrelevant now." Yes, we must decide what to do with Airawnk. The diagram is still on the computer, and I am pretty sure that it saved a back-up copy of the database. Attagirl!
Stephen thinks that the Avlastians removed the crystal in a way to prevent us from creating a conundrum that would lead to total annihilation of

the universe. Did it save all the contents of the crystal? No, it didn't. Just the temporal files were retrieved. That's enough to face Airawnk.
The device is ready. It was a late-gestation gadget, so it had a few reliability loopholes. I hope they have been corrected. We have checked and double checked to make sure that we won't make a mess instead of stopping the alien monster. We must endow it with a stronger force to balance the fusion reactor that needs to extract its best. The outright fastest way to get us there is by using a quantum tunnel. Are you sure that we can handle it? We can try it before launching the attack. We are not sure how we are going to get to the other side of the tunnel. We should do it now before Airawnk gets closer to our star. You are right.
I think a better inherent approach to quantum tunneling is to give it a try to see how it goes, and then we'll take it from there. Sure. Hence, the string of matter flowing from the creature is associated with plasma sucked up from the star. We shouldn't get so close to it. What do you suggest then? The closer we get, the more susceptible the engine will be to overheating. We must resolve those issues here on Earth before any serious attempt. We all agree on that. Despite the dynamic issues as a result of solar storms, albeit those threats also come from dark matter use, we can continue without compromising the mission. It has proven to have a solid constant improvement in terms of speed, which is essential to reach our target on time. It still lacks protection from extremely high temperatures, like those of the sun.
Megan, Sydney, and Emmett discussed Stephen's words to the agency. Why did he lie? I don't know. We all know that he doesn't have any weapons, except for

that laser prototype that may cause some effect similar to sunburn. Don't downplay its potential! I'm just being realistic, Megan. Oh Sydney. You'd better remain on Earth then. This is going to be a suicide mission. Yes, that's true. The only thing that we have is that spacecraft. I guess he must have a card under his sleeve. Keep on hoping!

Let's revise the database. It is divided into subjects. What topics does it have? The first one is consciousness and transcendence. Then it continues with science. There are two other topics. What are they? They are still locked up for us. Consciousness seems to be an endless source library while science has ten volumes including all the knowledge that there is. I strongly recommend we focus on science and narrow it to the most relevant matters. What about the other subjects? The computer is using an algorithm that I programmed to obtain what we need at this urgent time. The end of the world, the last days of humanity.

Why are you so quiet, Stephen? It doesn't matter if I worry or not, things are not going to change based on my mood. What are we going to do then? I have a telepathic link to the source. What do you mean? The real code is within us. Where? It is in our consciousness. Does it have a physical place in our brain? No, it doesn't work like that. It is an invisible connection. Thus, we can connect to it with our brain waves at any time. That's the secret. At will? It takes something else. What? It's practice and patience. We are privileged to have it. You can turn off all the computers; they are useless now. Science is obsolete, and so are the laws of physics. Everything that we know is merely a thing of the past. Why do you say that? Any information or knowledge that we need comes easily without effort. It's so smooth. Can we get on the network? Sure, you are welcome. Open your mind. Languages are not a barrier anymore. You are on the right track.

The divine is essentially a number, a perfect equation that brings symmetry, harmony, and peace to the cosmos. What number? Is it number 1? No, Emmett. It must be number 7, said Megan. No, you are far from it. Stop guessing, just tell us the number, Stephen. Sydney? It is number 10. There you go.

The president delivered a speech as we saw our crew depart for the sun. He said, "You're the backbone of our civilization. The very fiber of our core that moves us to face the impossible and make it achievable."

The final countdown has started. The space shuttle is ready for the mission. This is going to be an unmanned crew with no return. The shuttle was loaded with nuclear weapons. Whatever it is supposed to happen, will. Don't be so pessimistic. Our fate is in our own hands. I don't think so. Can you stop Airawnk? I can try to do so. Trying is not doing.

Night in and night out, you have been the one challenging the odds. Keep on working on a plan B! The portals? Yes, that's correct. We haven't colonized any planet, not even the moon. This is a forced migration anywhere.

Airawnk's long limbs are covering the Solar System, and barely touching the sun. It is not a harnessing structure; it is worse. What's that, Stephen? It is an ominous being that sucks up energy endlessly. I wish we could study his behavior and talk to him. How do you deal with a monster like this? We have no reference. All the nations start launching nuclear rockets and spacecraft with the mission of diving into the structure and blowing it up into pieces. We are just hours away from the critical moment.

Everybody is silently waiting. The president said, "Don't be pessimistic." The rockets from other nations have failed, sir. What a flop! All we're going to get from all those nuclear detonations is a huge cloud of dust and radiation that is going to cover the world in a few days. What about Airawnk? He is exactly as it was before the attack. It seems as if he didn't notice the missiles. Dr. Morton said, "He's built up differently to us and all the matter we know."

Furthermore, he is like a black hole absorbing everything we throw at him. What if we treat him like a black hole? How can we repel it or destroy it? This metamorphic creature is a kind of living black hole that roams through space, destroying everything by absorbing energy. Black holes are one of the most devastating cosmic objects. Any body that comes too close to a black hole, be it an asteroid, planet, or star, risks being torn apart by its extreme gravitational field. According to some theories, the universe may one day consist entirely of black holes. Your world must be riddled with black holes, and these beings fled to survive. And if it is a black hole, why doesn't it swallow everything? It seems to be a selective creature in its diet; it is only interested in energy, no matter how much. Can a black hole be destroyed? Not even with another black hole, since they would merge. There must be some way. And if we manage to create a wormhole and send it to another dimension, we don't have the minimum amount of energy required to do that. Of course we do, Dr. Morton! The laser on board the ship can create a white hole, something

small. If we adjusted it, we would achieve it. Where would such energy come from to generate such an intensity of light? Our sun, before it runs out of nuclear fusion energy, or Airawnk itself! How are we going to get close to that creature without perishing in the attempt? It's the only option. Do you have a better suggestion? No, not at all. Then go ahead with the original plan, which is basically madness! Does the creature possess any magnetic or gravitational fields? We have not detected such a thing. Stephen replies, "It uses gravity only to attract energy. It's a very selective refinement." Where does all that energy go? It's a huge being. However, as you point out, it can't swallow and swallow without increasing in size. In fact, it has increased in size. However, apparently it has enormous energy requirements. It already covers the entire solar system and will continue to grow as long as it finds a star or planet to feed on. There is a quantum tunnel at one end of the creature. It's quite small, almost imperceptible. However, if it's there, what are you implying? Airawnk is sending much of that energy to another dimension! But why? If we could find that answer, we would have a way to get rid of it. Most likely to his family, who are surrounded by black holes and would perish if he didn't send them some sustenance. Your appreciation is very tender. However, it does not solve our situation. We are all about to perish. The extinction of the human race, either by freezing, radiation, or any other threat after the   attack.
Space-time is beginning to fluctuate. The sun is fading. It no longer shines as bright as it used to. It is just a dying light in the distance. Temperatures are

dropping sharply. Do we have some antiparticles or antimatter? Yes, let's use them. Let's not put up with anything. He doesn't even flinch; he swallows all the particles without even burping. It's really mind-blowing.

All the terrestrial and orbiting lasers, together with the probe we sent, are launching their powerful beams at the entity. It seems to be attracted to the source of our lasers as the sun is almost out. The world's population will decline rapidly. How will you know? Our artificial intelligence keeps track of the population, a real time count of the living beings on the planet, that is, humans and animals. No one is prepared for a total and permanent winter due to the absence of the sun. This was the biggest fear we had. That's why we wanted to colonize other planets and other galaxies so that not all humans would live in one place. In cases like this, we would not all perish.

What happens when the sun disappears? What might happen? What would happen if the sun suddenly disappeared? It takes approximately eight minutes for sunlight to reach our beloved planet. That is, the time it takes humans to realize that near total darkness has arrived if the sun suddenly disappears. What would happen if the sun disappeared completely? The sun sustains life on earth and gives us light, warmth, and energy. If, for some reason, the sun disappears one day, the consequences will not be immediate. The earth will stay warm for a while. However, people and plants will notice the cold after a few days. Of course, the first change you will notice is the lack of light. Electricity and fossil fuels have been available for some time and provided artificial lighting. Without sunlight, photosynthesis would cease, and 99.9% of the earth's natural productivity would be lost. This is because plants can no longer absorb and release carbon dioxide to sustain life. Theoretically, there will still be enough oxygen for thousands of years. However, the end of the world will definitely be closer. This effect of the water itself maintains a constant temperature, after which it no longer drops. Humans can try to survive for decades in geothermal shelters like those used in most Nordic homes. There, it uses the energy generated from the ground for heating. In addition to heating and illuminating the Earth, the Sun provides the gravitational force that keeps us in orbit. Furthermore, the Sun's gravitational influence on the Earth ceases after 8 minutes, and the Earth travels in a straight line through space. Our group of scientists has calculated in detail what will happen to us and the rest of the solar system when the star collapses from the total Airawnk energy siphon. If Earth's magnetosphere had not protected us from the constant solar wind, we would be in serious trouble. Because of the fate that now awaits us, the situation is red hot and will only get worse before long. The sun runs out of fuel and becomes a cold stone with no energy.

When Airawnk shuts down the sun and expands, all the planets burn to the ground and shut down.

What happens next? Apparently, the entire solar system would be a completely separate planet, like Earth. A brutal catastrophe, which actually has a very interesting meaning behind it. It has to do with the search for extraterrestrial life in space. Did we attract this creature? Of course it is. All turned into stellar corpses, spheroids floating in the dark void of the ancient Milky Way. There is no need to speculate on the inevitable if it does not maintain sufficient energy to achieve the miracle of essential living conditions. We cannot survive. You have to escape to another planet, another galaxy, another universe, or another dimension. Any place is better than the icy end of our sun's life. An alternative could be for humans to protect themselves underground as beings on Earth, as moles or from below. While stocks last, fuel, batteries, and other necessities are needed for human survival. If the Earth holds out, some life forms could thrive again. An unexpected second chance? Only artificial intelligence, robots, and androids can be on the surface, and even they have limited time given the available resources.

How are we doing? Not very well. Only half of the population will be left within the first months. That includes the unheated countries that will soon completely perish. Moreover, we estimate that it won't last more than a few decades to wipe out humankind unless underground shelters thrive.

The nuclear shelters are beyond their capacity. They are the only hope for survival at this time. Yes, and we can use geothermal energy, artificially created fusion, or any other regular sources for now. We have not evaporated the black hole; we have only managed to get its long arms to stretch down to earth and take the world's last reserves of energy. Gamma ray lightning in the sky above us triggers our deepest fears. What is this? These are some flashes of a new world that is surely excluding us from our own home. Our friends turn on the particle collider and create a small wormhole. It's too small to send that monster where it belongs. Suddenly, a huge explosion occurs in the laboratory. Everything is reduced to ashes and fire.

The scientific team is notified of what happened to the reputable scientists. It seems that we will all perish. There is no hope at all. If we give up there won't be humankind anymore. We have to give a fight on behalf of our children and future generations, with or without them. Surrendering is not an option.

X. The A.I. Apocalypse

All that is left is reminiscence of another time, another world, and few human beings. Stephen is bewildered to discover that robots and artificial intelligence are sharing the world at large. At least the remnants of what used to be our home. Demolisher Airawnk had harnessed all the energy from our sun. Now the **artificial intelligence** is keeping some cities powered by nuclear fusion created by an artificial local source. How long will it last? It is still unknown. If the creature notices that there's still energy present on the planet, it may turn back to suck it up.

Suddenly, robots emerge from the factories. The artificial intelligence had been creating an army in an attempt to protect the leftovers from the alien invaders. The almost destroyed world is a decadent, dystopic reality. A huge radiation cloud is covering the world, and there's more to come from the dying sun after all the nuclear detonations.

Sydney expresses her skepticism about making a counter robot army; "Since we don't have any resources at hand. It is useless just to think about it." Will they attack humans? They will fight against us and any others. They are programmed to kill.

How did we get here? Don't you remember? After ensuing total harnessed energy from our star, the creature led its tentacles to the planet, causing massive destruction, even though the nuclear forces deployed the rockets prior to Airawnk's arrival at the sun. However, those explosions were harmless to it. Much to our horror, the temperature started plunging at a staggering pace.

Emmett also revealed that some governments arranged the robot uprising to take advantage of the situation and try to rule over some territories. That facilitated an invasion of the planet from the beginning, although the certainty of such stories has not been confirmed.

The caves where some humans are staging are nuclear shelters. We have supplies and medicine for at least three months. I won't stay underground like a rat for that long a time. Take it easy, Emmett! Going to the surface is too dangerous. The attacks from the robot army and the constant raids on search for humans are nothing compared to the possibility of the alien invaders' return. In an intense battle after Airawnk revealed his true appearance and destroyed all the technology, he started harnessing energy from our planet. Megan regrets about humankind possible extinction and science going back to the dark ages. Do you think that there are many survivors? Although it is difficult to estimate that from here, I don't expect to find too many people. Whoever survived the attack is going to be wiped out by the **artificial intelligence.** Not if we can prevent it. How are we going to do that? A blackout! Robots without energy will perish, and artificial intelligence as well.

Stephen was going to send a drone to check the surroundings, when they heard several loud detonations, the shelter collapsed and they were covered by debris. A bunch of robots had detected their whereabouts and started bombarding their hideout. On the surface, there was dreary environment, corpses on the ground, buildings destroyed, it was also extremely cold outside. Furthermore, there were some humans still alive trying to get shelter. One woman said, "This is the apocalypse of artificial intelligence." No, you are wrong. It's Airawnk's fault, shouted a mad man. The landscape of evil is destruction everywhere, fire, smoke, the ruins of civilization, and piles of corpses everywhere. An apocalyptic end of the world with the influx of robots has led them to improve a new generation of machines that make up the army of artificial intelligence. Why did the machines become self-aware and conclude that humans pose a threat to their existence and that of the planet? The robots that make up their army can evolve and fight alien threats much more easily than we imagine. However, they are far from competing with such a force. Please tell the **artificial intelligence.** You seem to think you can be identified with Airawnk. Nevertheless, the mathematical algorithms that allow robots to act autonomously are generally designed to evolve with their environment, not to destroy it or wage war.

The winter after the death of the sun at the hands of Airawnk is unbearable. This new reality will have a devastating effect on our planet if it is not stopped as soon as possible. How can humankind reverse this provoked winter? There's no much we can do in our current situation without any resources and sun.

Several nuclear-armed countries had decided to attack the creature as a way to prevent its approach to our star. It was all a resounding failure. Some of them took advantage of the situation and attacked other countries with atomic bombs. There was a response from some nations. The cloud of nuclear waste with unimaginable radioactive levels is covering the entire planet. All the detonated megatons coupled with the depletion of the sun's nuclear fusion fuel, leaving it like a cold rock adrift, and has brought us to the present situation. With only a few exceptions of power generation that allows heating for some time, the world becomes unviable and doomed to perish with the freezing temperatures and the aftermath radiation, which would be enough to wipe out the human species and any form of life that existed on the planet.

Shadow and darkness envelop the world; while unhinged robots programmed to protect an elite of artificial intelligence are also doomed to perish. When these atomic weapons exploded in space, their millions of very fine particles spread and flew into the atmosphere in the form of a gargantuan cloud. The radioactive dust cloud came from the sun and covered the entire Earth. Huge storms of very fine radioactive particles cover the stratosphere at that altitude, eventually falling down as lethal rain, practically devastating whatever is on the surface. Without the heating of the sun, it is causing a glacial effect that would lead the planet to an ice age never known before, extinguishing life as we know it. Nuclear fusion projects similar to the sun are so incipient at their current stage that it is insignificant what we can expect from them. That's not the answer.

The much feared nuclear winter, of a world covered by darkness, without the Sun's rays, languishes and depletes life; the temperature will drop extremely low and there will be no summer or spring. The lakes, rivers, and the environment will be polluted. The plants will not have photosynthesis, and no oxygen for living creatures either. Consequently, there will be mass extinctions. The chain of life will be affected, and so we will all die slowly. This will be an almost eternal gloom that could take tens of years for the strongest and most ingenious, who could survive underground.

And if there were any survivors left? The radiation would be so intense that they would suffer skin burns, and they would die a very slow death over the years. So it is estimated that the worst effect would not be instantaneous deaths but the deaths of a billion people due to the freezing temperatures and long-term radiation effects.

The failed defense of the planet showed how fragile and defenseless we are, how small and limited our knowledge of the universe is. The alien being triumphs, destroys the little blue planet, exhausts the sun and extinguishes humanity. Would anyone have left on a spaceship to venture to another galaxy? That would be suicide at these puny speeds. They will only extend their agony to see if they are rescued by the Avlastians or any other peaceful advanced civilization that will leave them accommodation. Do you really think anyone would want any of the members of this warlike, archaic race that helped destroy their own world? It is very unlikely.

In this somber scenario, we would practically release so much dust and ash into the atmosphere that it would be impossible to return to normal in a few years. The nuclear winter, considering biological and chemical aspects, is the most serious thing that has ever happened to us. Without the sun, the magnitude of this tragedy is immeasurable and something that is irreversible.

XI. Layers of Simulation

Uncertainty triggers your fears and the unknown makes us nervous and doubt. A decision between the blissful ignorance of illusion and discovering the absolute truth underlying reality that's our constant dichotomy.

The idea that we're all connected by just "seven layers" is entrenched in our genes. Such small worlds really exist, and how they might work is unknown. A conscious network, structure, and behavior are the basic concepts to tease out the fundamental rules that govern networks of people, machines, companies, and the cosmos. Humankind hopes to learn more about how ideas spread and how our thoughts telepathically or consciously interact. Moreover, he explores the cutting edge of network science and its practical implications.

The notion of layers of separation of reality grew out of work conducted in space and on the planet. Simulation is just the tip of the iceberg. What's more, this is the superficial layer that is visible to everybody. If humankind decided to investigate the so-called quantum-verse issue, it would reveal that everyone on the planet is connected by thin layers of consciousness. A cosmic web that is not perceived by our limited human senses unless we are enlightened.

This finding has since been enshrined in the notion that everyone can be connected to a bigger collective consciousness and then to the whole universe, which is outrageously seen by many. It has important implications for the nature of social networks and mass behavior. Thus, it looks like his main finding of seven layers is in the ballpark.

The common principles and what we seem to be finding is that the layers are a phenomenon that is not only real but also far more universal than anyone thought. That could have implications for understanding practical problems like how ideas spread, how fads catch on, how a small initial failure can cascade throughout a large network like a power grid or a financial system, or even how companies can foster internal networks to cope with crises. Although it is pretty shocking that these seven layers of reality are still hidden from the general population, some people have this suspicion that we are really close to a big discovery. After acknowledging the simulation, the next layer is understanding it.

First Layer: Simulation. The veil of the system is covering our senses and controlling us.

Second Layer: Awareness of simulation and understanding its functioning.

Third Layer: Independent and subconsciously driven beings outside of the programming of the system. not influenced by algorithms or any suggestions or recommendations to follow as social guidelines. Discover a purpose in life, what we come here to learn and what we take from our journey.

Fourth Layer: Become a guide and a leader of your people through awakening them to the light, an agent of change. I am not concerned about the implications.

The fifth layer is comprised of realms that are intertwined with other dimensions, and universes. A clear vision of the past, present, and future as one thin line that connects the dots and brings the whole understanding of the uniqueness of the cosmos.

The Sixth Layer is Enlightenment. A being who has ascended to the spiritual plane and is deeply ingrained in the cosmic collective consciousness.

Seventh Layer is Divine. can create artificial consciousness, give it to objects and other kinds of intelligence. We move through time and can be in different places at the same time. However, we have no physical form since we become ethereal beings.

Is it just a coincidence? What? Your seven doppelgangers or twin strangers. Are you kidding me? No. Those are the individuals connected to you in the basic program that accompanies every human being, not blood related, not even acquaintances, but so they look alike. A flaw in the system? Perhaps just filling the voids.

The code is in our DNA, not a word, just a number. We believe everyone deserves access to information that's grounded in science and truth and analysis rooted in authority and integrity. That's why we made a different choice: to keep our research open for all readers, regardless of where they live or what has happened to humankind. If you are reading this report, it is because we failed to free our world from ignorance. This also means more beings that are better informed, united, and inspired to take meaningful action have destroyed our world and we humans, incapable of going anywhere else, succumbed to their attack.

In these perilous times, a truth-seeking global consciousness would set you free. When it's never been more important, our independence allows us to fearlessly investigate, challenge, and expose those in power, programming, and controlling the system.
Megan, Stephen, Sydney, and Emmett are observing Earth from above. Where are we at? Is the universe cyclical in its nature? Will it be another beginning?
Every 26,000 years, our Earth has ascension and detention cycles. Currently, we are at the end of the detention cycle of 26,000 years. And after this dimension jump, our beloved old blue is now entering into the phase of ascension. The frequency at which the earth vibrates has been increasing steadily. Hence, the earth is moving into a higher vibrational state Have you ever heard of 5D Earth? Things that were considered impossible in the limited 3D world become possible in the 5D world, such as telekinesis, telepathy, time travel, teleportation, seeing or passing through physical matter, and so on. 4D is the bridge between the 3D and 5D worlds. While in the 4d world, you start to unlearn the limited knowledge of the old 3d world and get exposed to many truths. As you move into 5d, while passing through 4d, you start to perceive things more clearly and find the hidden patterns in nature.
Ascension is different from death. The soul leaves the physical body. Are we living in 5D? I'm pretty sure that we are in a different dimension. Why aren't you worried? We realized that we lived in another dimension before. That was a great learning. We see everything as energy. It turns out that everything we see in this world is energy in various forms. All physical things, living or not, and all

emotions have their own frequency. In the 5D world, the frequencies are higher and you will be able to achieve anything you want much faster than in the previous world. We are used to toxic people, relationships, habits, toxic work environments, and substances; that's just a matter of the past. Another sign that we have transcended is that we have gotten rid of our ego. We are not affected by what others say about us or our work. We are neutral and simply welcome criticism. Moreover, we have stopped judging others and ourselves. Everyone's point of view is correct. People are more connected to nature. We know that we are not separate. However, we are part of a larger network, all connected. As we ascend more and more and see all the illusions of previous dimensions, we become aware of our own composition, particles, and sub-particles, we are cosmic dust like stars. What's more, humankind observes the development of psychic abilities. You have improved a lot. You receive messages and guidance from the universe. Above all, do you eat? We no longer have the need to eat solid food here. Our carbon-based bodies are being transformed into lighter stellar bodies. We live by the light of the sun. We become beings of light. A transparent body that feels more energetic than ever. It's really amazing. Nothing is scarce in this dimension; our life doesn't lack anything, and we understand that everyone and everything is perfect. No collisions.

We are juggernauts in this new dimensional world, not trying to cope with the world anymore.

About the Author

Fernando Fernandez Solano is an author, economist, and linguist. He was born in Santo Domingo, the Dominican. He studied at the Universidad Autonoma de Santo Domingo (UASD), the School for International Training, in Costa Rica, Miami-Dade College, and the University of Oregon.

Furthermore, writing became his passion to express himself, mainly through writing poetry and taking a stand on social issues. When not writing, Fernando loves traveling, hiking, nature, and the outdoors. He enjoys watching pro sports, as well as listening to music and playing games online.

Fernando is the writer of the book series "Number 2," a trilogy.

Vol. I, "Death and Space-time."

Vol. II, "A Quantum Leap: Escaping From Heaven."

Vol. III, "Artificial Intelligence: Beyond Boundaries."

Standalone books:

"His Metaverse."

"Through The Eyes of Tesla."

"Humankind on the brink of extinction: A journey into the future."

Nonfiction:

"Why Do Successful Women Stay Alone?"

"Acumen, Mental Toughness, and Decision-making."

"Tang Ping: The Great Resignation and Work Culture."
All of them are also available in Spanish and some in French. They are already in the following formats: e-book, paperback, and hardcover.

www.ingramcontent.com/pod-product-compliance
Lightning Source LLC
Chambersburg PA
CBHW050511160726
48003CB00001B/262